THE
EGRET

A novella by

RUSSELL
HILL

Pleasure Boat Studio: A Literary Press
Seattle, Washington

ISBN 978-0-912887-69-2
Library of Congress Control Number: 2017956626

Cover egret painting: Timothy Goss, timgosswatercolors.com
Cover and book design: Lauren Grosskopf
Editors: Jack Estes
Jeff Welker

Pleasure Boat Studio books are available through your favorite bookstore
and through the following:
SPD (Small Press Distribution) 800-869-7553
Baker & Taylor 800-775-1100
Ingram 615-793-5000
Amazon.com and bn.com
and through
PLEASURE BOAT STUDIO: A LITERARY PRESS
www.pleasureboatstudio.com
Seattle, Washington

Contact Lauren Grosskopf, Publisher
Email: Pleasboatpublishing@gmail.com

Your eye shall not pity. It shall be life for life, eye for eye, tooth for tooth, hand for hand, foot for foot.

Deuteronomy 19-21

THE
EGRET

THE OCEAN

CHAPTER 1

The tide was out, leaving a stretch of mudflat from the edge of the sandy beach out to where the water began. It was silent, six o'clock in the morning, the motel behind me quiet, no one else up, only an occasional crow squawk from across the highway. Nothing in front of me except the bay that lapped at the edge of the mud, forty yards off. A breeze ruffled the water beyond the edge.

An egret came toward me, low, its wingtips touching the surface and then it splayed its wings, came upright, and settled its long legs into the water. It folded its wings and remained motionless. I watched it. Its shadow against the mud was like two apostrophes touching each other, a mirror image. It did not move. Then, slowly it bent its head, canting it to one side, looking intently at something beneath the surface. Something down there had moved, and it waited, head bent, still, motionless as sleep, motionless as death. And it was death for whatever had moved. Some tiny fish or a mollusk or a mud worm. Something that was alive and would not be alive in a few moments. I waited to see the egret strike. But it did not move. It maintained its motionless presence, waiting, waiting. I realized that it could wait longer than I could. And it came to me that the thing that was the target had no idea that death was poised above it.

The worm continued to work its way through the mud or the tiny fish finned searching for something to eat while the thing that would eat it waited patiently for the right moment.

And that was it. Be the egret. Be the creature that was silent and motionless, and when it struck the strike would be deadly and quick and what I needed to do was to practice patience. Practice waiting. Practice holding myself in readiness, waiting for the right moment. There was no point in rushing in. If the egret moved, the worm would suddenly bury itself, the minnow dart away beyond the reach of the sharp bill. Wait, I told myself. Wait for the moment when he was unaware that I was there; wait until he moved as carelessly as that tiny fish.

The egret lifted one leg, a millimeter at a time until the foot was clear of the water, and then the egret placed the foot in the water, lowered its leg until it was no longer bent, and it was a few inches forward, head still canted, eye seeing the thing that would be snatched up in a single thrust. I could hear that crow calling out again. I did not move. How long would the egret wait? Probably longer than I could stay motionless, watching.

I heard a noise and turned. A man approached, an older man, slightly bent, and he held a leash and a dog, a small dog that stopped, bristling when it saw me. It barked several times and the man told it to be quiet, pulled at the leash. I looked back at the egret, but it was gone.

"Up early?" the man said.

"Yes, it's quiet at this time."

"Sorry about Ralph. He's friendly, but he has to announce himself." Now he was close enough so that the dog came toward me, tugging at the leash, and it barked again.

"He won't bite," the man said.

How often have I heard that one? He won't bite and the

child stretches out a hand to pet the dog and suddenly the teeth snatch at the outstretched fingers. "But he never does that!" the owner protests while the child howls, clutching its hand. This dog sniffed at my shoes, and I thought for a moment that it would raise a leg and piss on me, but it waited, I suppose, for me to pet it.

"Sweet dog," I said. I like dogs. This one reminded me of a dog that we had, my daughter's dog, a feisty little schnauzer, but when it got old and deaf and its hindquarters didn't work right it began to lash out at people who approached it from behind. It couldn't hear them and it lashed out at the unknown. Eventually it got to the point where it couldn't function all that well and I took it to the vet. "I can stitch it together," he said. "It's unraveling, but you won't be doing it any favor if you have me do that "

"So it's come to the end?" I asked.

"I can do it for you," he said.

"No, I need to do this myself." By then my daughter was dead, and Trigger was the only thing left alive that was connected to her, if you discounted me and my wife, who had left me three years before.

"The humane society does it," he said, and I drove out there and filled out the papers and sat with Trigger in the lobby and then a nice young woman came out. She reminded me a bit of my daughter. She took Trigger and said, "It won't be long," and then she came back with the papers and I went out to my truck and sat behind the wheel and cried. I cried for the old dog and I cried for my daughter.

CHAPTER 2

Detective Robert Fuller came to the house late in the afternoon. When he knocked on the door I was having my second vodka over ice, a ritual I have every afternoon. I knew Fuller from the accident. My daughter was coming home from an afternoon at Heart's Desire Beach on the Point Reyes peninsula and when she came around a curve, there was the Ford Expedition, over the center line, cutting the corner and it struck her car a glancing blow. The huge SUV hardly wavered, but my daughter's little car was airborne, sending it pinwheeling into the edge of Tomales Bay. Those were the words of the truck driver who saw the accident. "The car pinwheeled and landed on its roof in the edge of the bay," he said. "I stopped, but the car that clipped her just kept going."

Fuller was with the Marin County Sheriff's Department and had been in charge of the investigation and he hadn't found the car or the driver. All he had was her death. And that had destroyed my marriage. I was devastated by her death, a bright girl in her freshman year at SF State, on the way back from a Point Reyes beach after a day with friends, and some sonofabitch came around a corner and clipped her car, sending it pinwheeling into the bay. Pinwheeling. A Fourth of July verb. It was the verb that the truck driver who witnessed the accident used on the police report. She drowned in the upside down car. My whole life pinwheeled as well, and eventually my wife grew tired of my grief.

We tried counseling but there was this big hole in my life and I must confess that I was no good at the group sessions at the Catholic Social Services, couples arranged in a circle trying to deal with the deaths of their children. I was not good at it and Andrea gave up on me. I didn't blame her. The sessions were designed so that each couple shared their story. There were couples whose child had overdosed on drugs. One couple described an automobile accident, a teenage driver going too fast over White's Hill, lost control, plunged over the edge of the road and the car rolled until it was a crushed wreckage, the occupants dead.

The facilitator of the group was a middle aged woman with a ball point pen in the bun of hair that was tightly wound over her forehead, and she kept saying that it was good to talk things out. Put your grief into words, she said. But I could not put words to my daughter's death. She had hung, trapped, upside down while her car sank in Tomales Bay, and the water rose until it enveloped her. I could imagine her lifting her head as the water rose and when I was asked how my daughter died, I could only say that she had drowned. My wife began to correct me, saying, No, it was not an ordinary drowning, but before she could explain, I rose and left the room.

I had nightmares in which I dove into the water to pry open the door of an upside down car, hearing my daughter's voice bubbling through the water. My wife moved to the guest room. She said I shouted in my sleep, thrashed so much that I struck her.

Things came back to me in a rush at odd times of the day. I spent time in my garage making birdhouses. She loved birds and kept a log of birds that she had spotted. I still had that little black book with notations: *A cardinal! So red that it was unreal. San Anselmo Park, October 16, 5:00 p.m. How wonderful!*

I sometimes pictured her on the dock at Bodega Bay where I had taken her to fish for perch when she was not yet a teenager, her face lighting up when a wriggling perch came up to the railing. Soccer games. I took time off work to watch her run down the field, long-legged, a fluid movement and when she went off to SF State, I drove her to the dorm, carried her box of things up to her room, helped her to move in, met her roommate, a black girl from Compton. I bought her the Toyota and she brought her roommate to the house for dinner, a sweet girl who played soccer as well, but was not good enough to be on the SF State women's soccer team.

I remembered times when she was out late in high school and I had met some of the friends who hung out with her, some boys that I had reservations about, and I waited up, listening for the front door that told me she had made it safely back to the house. My wife was asleep. She'll be all right, she repeatedly told me.

Fuller shook my hand, and I asked if he wanted a coffee or a drink.

"What are you drinking?" he asked.

"Vodka over ice."

"Not my style."

"I've got some scotch."

"That would be nice!"

"To what do I owe this visit?"

I poured him a scotch and he took a sip, then placed the glass on the coffee table.

"I've found the sonofabitch who clipped your kid."

"You found him? You're going to arrest him?"

"No. I know who he is, but I haven't got enough evidence to arrest him."

I was stunned.

Fuller took out a small notebook, laid it on the coffee table and opened it.

"That was three years ago," I said. "I thought you gave up on it."

"No. That's a fault of mine. I struggle along, and some cases solve themselves and some of them drift along without a clue to help solve things, and I'm like some old dog chewing on a bone. I've been doing this twenty-five years. It doesn't get easier, it gets harder."

"So what happened this time?"

"You remember that we put out an alert to body shops about a Ford Expedition that might need body work on the right side?"

"But nothing came back."

"That's right. But last week there's a guy doing an audit at Gotelli's Body Work in San Rafael, a routine examination of the books for taxes, and he comes across our BOLO. And apparently nobody did anything with it. So here he is, with all these old records, and he's curious, which is a stroke of luck for me, so he checks it out and sure enough there's a black Ford Expedition that comes in two days after the accident date, and it gets fixed and the sonofabitch comes in and pays them in cash and drives off. There's no insurance, the name he gives them turns out to be a phony and the address in Vallejo doesn't exist. But of course the body shop takes down the VIN number of the car, that's routine. And a check with the DMV tells us who bought the sucker. It's only a year old when it gets fixed, so chances are that this is the original owner." He traced something in his notebook with his index finger.

"Earl Anthony Winslow. 221 Carmel Drive, Ross, California."

"That's an expensive address."

"Unless he lives in the chauffeur's quarters over the garage."

"So you go there and you arrest the sonofabitch."

"No. What I have is a three-year old car repair. He'll claim that he didn't want the accident to go on his insurance, which is why he paid cash. I can't connect that damage to your daughter's car. The damaged parts are long gone. He'll make up some cockamamie story about why he used a false name. There's nothing there that I can use to make a direct connection to your daughter's death."

"But you think it's him?"

"Two DUI convictions. A summer cottage in Inverness, not two miles from where he sideswiped the kid's car."

"Why are you telling me this?"

"I have two daughters. One of them is married, two grandkids. The other one is a doctor. She spends time in Third World countries fixing the bodies of poor kids. When they were growing up, I sweated out every Saturday might. They were both a bit on the wild side, parties and nights on beaches with a keg of beer and boys that I would just as soon have arrested and I lived in fear that something would happen to them. But nothing did. Sometimes I think it's all just a matter of luck. What I know is this." He paused, closed his notebook, picked up his glass and sipped at the scotch. "If some motherfucker sideswiped the car of one of my daughters, and pitched her into the bay and kept on going, I would have hunted down the asshole and I would have put a bullet into his head."

"Are you saying I should find this prick and kill him?"

"I'm not saying anything of the kind. I'll continue to work on the case, but it's a cold case, and my boss won't be happy if I spend too much time on it. I'll find that truck driver, if he's findable, and ask him some more questions. But it's unlikely that I'll find anything that concretely ties Earl Winslow to this. What you do is your own business." He sipped at the scotch again.

"You're sure it's him?"

"I'm going to talk to him. Ask him about the repair to his car. Ask to see the car if he still has it. See how he reacts. It's been three years. It will be interesting to see how he reacts when I show up with questions."

"And you'll let me know?"

"You'll be the first person I talk to."

I could feel the blood rising in my neck, feel a sudden agitation in my body. When I looked at my hands, I could see that I was clasping and unclasping them, forming fists.

"Maybe it's all just coincidence. Maybe the damage to his car has nothing to do with that hit and run. But the truck driver, according to the field interview, was sure it was a black Expedition. Driven by a man. And two days later a black Expedition gets fixed, paid for with cash, a phony name and address. Rich bastard who has a house out at Inverness, and a record of driving under the influence. I don't like coincidence. In all my years, I've never found one that held up." He finished his scotch.

"Thanks for the drink. I'll be in touch. Don't do anything foolish."

I stood, shook his hand. His face was lined and he looked at least fifteen years older than me. Which put him in his sixties. He looked tired.

"Thanks," I said.

"I didn't give you anything," he said. "Maybe some grief. Like I said, don't do anything foolish. Maybe I should amend that. Don't do anything. I'll be in touch."

He left and I stood looking at the closed door. I would find 221 Carmel Drive in Ross. I would find Earl Anthony Winslow. I would see what he looks like. I would find out all I could about him. And if I were convinced that he was the one, then I would do something. Something foolish, no doubt. But I had spent the last three years during which there was never a day when I didn't think about the death of my daughter. Fuller had no idea what his news had done to me. It had struck a match to the fuse.

CHAPTER 3

On the anniversary of my daughter's death I take a room at the Tomales Bay Resort and I visit the spot where her car landed. The resort is a quiet one in the spring. Summer is a different matter. The Lodge has a small marina and the crowds come to their boats. The sailboats are all center boarders now that the bay has silted up as much as it has. At low tide the boats in the marina sit on the mud.

My daughter and I came out here several times. I rented a small boat and we sailed toward Marshall, the rising afternoon wind heeling the boat so that one rail was almost in the water. She loved to hike out on the high side, yelling at me to come closer to the wind, drop the rail even farther. "Come on Dad! Bury it!"

That's where I was this weekend. I could imagine Earl Anthony Winslow driving his Ford Expedition out the two-lane road toward his vacation cottage. Traffic came quickly around the curves. The road was narrow. Every once in a while a big tanker truck came, either from Point Reyes Station or back from one of the dairy ranches scattered on the peninsula. Some of those ranches dated back to the 1850's.

I drove out to North Beach on the western side of the peninsula. The parking lot is close to the water, and the beach was empty. I walked down through the soft sand to stand at the edge of the water. The surf was its usual maelstrom of surging water. There was nothing between this beach and Japan. The beach shelves off dramatically, the sand dipping and the waves tumbling over each other, smashing up the slope, one on top of the next, the following waves surging over it all. It is a mass of churning, angry water, a constant roar, and people have died on this beach. The unwary Iowa tourist who wants to dip his or her feet into the Pacific comes down to the edge and suddenly a sneaker wave engulfs them to their knees and their feet slip in the dissolving sand and they are pulled under and when they surface, the water is a hundred feet deep, the mad cauldron of surf between them and the beach, and the undertow drags them out further and within minutes the icy water immobilizes them. Anyone foolish enough to plunge into the surf to save them drowns, too. One story was of a man's dog that got dragged into the surf. The man went after the dog, was dragged out, and drowned. 'The dog made it back to the beach.

I could imagine Earl Anthony Winslow in that surf. I could imagine watching him flail his arms, try to swim, only to be tumbled by the violent water, and he, too, would drown, just as my daughter did when her car pinwheeled into Tomales Bay. Perhaps Winslow would be foolish enough to come out to North Beach to watch the surf and perhaps he would be foolish enough to decide to get his feet wet and perhaps he would, like that unwary Iowa tourist, find himself sliding into the churning water

I found a log half buried at the high tide mark, and sat against it, letting the log take the brunt of the wind at my back. I watched the surf. It did not change.

I drove back into Point Reyes Station and stopped at the Old Western Saloon. It's one of those old fashioned small town saloons, and the men at the bar were workers from the dairy ranches and carpenters and the drivers of trucks for Toby's Barn, hauling sand and hay into Petaluma and Santa Rosa and San Rafael, and taking milk from the scattered ranches to Strauss Dairy where it would become butter and ice cream and milk for breakfast cereal. Nothing fancy about the Old Western. Beer and shots and a young bartender in a tee shirt and Tule elk antlers on the wall. The bang of cups and the calls for liar's dice resounded.

"Scotch on the rocks," I said, pushing a five spot onto the bar. He poured, no shot glass, a generous pour, gave me back a dollar. I pushed it back at him, and he pocketed it. No small talk.

The single main street through Point Reyes Station is Highway One, the highway that follows the California coast, and it was clogged with bike riders in spandex outfits, a few motorcycles and a stream of cars and pickups. The Bovine Bakery down the street had its usual cluster of people at the door. It had been a favorite of my daughter's. She and her friends came out on Sundays, had a pastry and a coffee, walked their dogs, went out to Limantour Beach or Heart's Desire and came back sunburned and wind blown. She had done it since she was a sophomore in high school. And when she turned sixteen and got her license, she became one of the drivers. Two years later she pinwheeled into Tomales Bay. And now I knew who had caused her to do that.

The drive back into Fairfax goes either through Samuel P. Taylor State Park, filled with redwoods, or up to Lake Nicasio and past the Rancho Nicasio bar and restaurant. This time I stopped there, went in and sat at the bar and ordered a BLT. The walls were filled with the heads of deer, a great ugly wild boar and another Tule elk, this one staring benignly down at the people eating their hamburgers and fries and BBQed oysters. I had another scotch and tried to imagine the death of Winslow. I could shoot him. Put a gun to his head and blow his brains out. But that was risky.

Police would investigate a death like that. He could have an accident, his car could plunge off the road but I didn't know how to engineer that. It was the stuff that you saw in TV shows. He could get poisoned, but that meant somehow getting at what he ate or drank. Or, and as I imagined this afternoon, he could go for a walk on North Beach and slip into the surf. And that would be the perfect death. A man who was taking a walk on a dangerous beach. A beach where people had died. A misstep and he would be found several miles away, washed up on the South Beach, and his car would still be in the North Beach parking lot where he had left it. And he would drown too, just like my daughter. He would find the water take him, try to breathe the heavy stuff, watch the water rise over him, know that he was dying, see the opaque world through the water and know that he was in the wrong element, an air-breathing creature who was trapped in the sea. And, like the young woman hanging upside down in the car, he would wonder why his life was ending too soon.

It required planning. Somehow I had to get him out there. Somehow it had to be in his car. And somehow I had to get myself back to Fairfax or at least to the Tomales Bay Lodge without anyone knowing that I had been involved in his death. I would be like the egret. I would wait for the right moment. I would wait until he was swimming beneath my beak, unaware that I was poised to end his life.

CHAPTER 4

Detective Fuller came back. He still looked tired, but he came in, accepted my offer of a scotch and sat on the couch, placing his little notebook on the coffee table.

"I assume you haven't done anything stupid," he said

"I'm not sure what you mean by stupid."

"I mean you haven't bought yourself a gun or hired a hit man,"

"Where would I find one of those?"

"On television."

He sipped the scotch, "This is good stuff," he said. "Better than what I'm used to."

"I don't have many expenses," I said. "No wife, no kid, no bad habits. At least not habits that cost a lot of money. So I buy good scotch, good vodka, good wine. My car is paid for. "

"But you've checked up on our buddy, haven't you?"

"Yes. I did some looking on the internet."

"And you drove by his house?"

"Yes. Nice place."

"Three Hispanic guys doing his lawn and his shrubs the day I was there. Three car garage. Fucking big house."

"He's well heeled. So what did you find out?"

"Nothing. At least nothing that I can use. I met with him, asked him about the car repair. He had the usual story, scraped it on a wall in a garage."

"What about the phony name?"

"Said he does that often. Doesn't want people to connect him. He's in big finance, wants to keep his private life private, so he keeps his name out of transactions that aren't important."

"You believe him?"

"No."

"What tells you that?"

"He was too quick with his answers. Here comes a Sheriff's detective, three years later. He ought to be vague. A car repair for a minor scrape three years ago? What the fuck is this all about? But the answers were rehearsed, like he'd been waiting for me. It's the kind of story that I hear all the time. Quick answers, a logical pattern. What the fuck are you asking me about this for? It's a rehearsed answer. I've heard enough of them to recognize one."

"So you're sure he's the one?"

"No, I'm not positive. If I had to put money on it, I'd put it on him. But I can't put the clamp on it. I can't say, yeah, he's the guy and know for sure that he's the perp. Everything fits, but I don't have that thing that would put him away. Paint scrapings from your daughter's car, a witness that put him out there, a license plate number from that truck driver. That's what I don't have, and there's not much chance that I'm going to get it."

"So he's going to get away with it?"

"I've found the truck driver. I'll interview him. Maybe he remembers something that will help."

"What if this bastard has an accident?"

"What kind of an accident?"

"I was thinking maybe he would take a walk on one of those Point Reyes beaches and maybe slip and get pulled out into the waves and drown."

"Jesus Christ! You're not serious!"

"It's just a thought."

"He's gonna go out there and wade in the surf and lose his footing and drown? You got any idea how that would happen?"

"No. I don't. Like I said, it's just a thought. One that I had yesterday."

"I don't want to arrest you. There's no reason for you to risk your own life and liberty for some asshole like him."

"If he's the one who sent my daughter to her death, then I've got nothing to lose."

"Jesus." He raised the scotch to his lips, took a sip. "I didn't hear that," he said.

CHAPTER 5

I went to a gun shop in Santa Rosa. It was the closest one to me. The others were in El Cerrito, Pacifica and San Bruno. The clerk was an older man, balding, shirt sleeves folded up, a bit of a neatly trimmed moustache, and he leaned over a case containing a variety of handguns.

"How can I help you, sir?"

"How would I go about buying a handgun?"

"Is it for yourself?"

"Yes."

"You ever own a gun before?"

"No, this is the first time. I'd like to have it around the house; we've had robberies lately, break-ins. I think I'd feel safer. What does it take?"

He handed me a brochure.

"You read this. It tells you what the safe handling requirements are, then you come back here and you take a test. It costs twenty-five bucks. You pass the test, you show me your driver's license, you bring something that shows you're a California resident, your PG&E bill, something like that. You demonstrate that you know how to safely handle a gun, then you pick one out, we fill out the papers, you pay me and you wait ten days to come back and pick it up. Assuming you don't have a criminal record. They'll check you out, make sure you're OK."

"What are the requirements for using the gun?"

"It's all in there," he said, pointing at the brochure. "You can keep it loaded at your house. You can't keep it loaded if you're in a car or on a public street. You can't carry it concealed. If you have it with you in your car, you gotta put it in the trunk, unloaded. Glove compartment or under the seat is a no-no. You want to look at one of these?"

"Sure."

He took a smaller gun out of the case and laid it on a felt pad on the counter.

"This is a Glock G43. Lightweight. It loads seven rounds. It's something that people buy when they want a lightweight weapon that handles easily."

I picked it up, gripped it, but I didn't raise it. I knew that much. Don't ever point a weapon at anybody. When I was a kid, I had a BB gun and my father was adamant about that.

"How do I learn to shoot something like this?"

"Gun range. There's a couple not too far from here. I can give you directions. Actually, we offer lessons. You make an appointment, somebody takes you through the drill."

I hoisted the gun again. It was light, black, deadly feeling, and I could imagine holding it to the temple of the asshole who had clipped my daughter's car. Holding the barrel to his head and pulling the trigger. I pulled the trigger and it clicked, and the clerk said, "This weapon is one of our best sellers."

I laid the gun back on the pad.

"I'll study this," I said, picking up the brochure.

Coming back down from Santa Rosa I thought about the idea of a gun. I thought about pressing it to the head of Earl Winslow, telling him to think about that girl hanging upside down in a car filling with water. And I was sure that I could kill him. But death by bullet seemed too quick, too painless.

On the other hand, a gun would be something that would get his attention if I wanted him to go out to Point Reyes to that empty beach. It might be something that would convince him. I needed to isolate him, use the gun to force him to drive out to that beach where the surf would swallow him. What I had to do was plan this carefully. Be like the egret. Be patient.

CHAPTER **6**

I got my daughter's bike out of the garage, put a small wrench in my pocket and took off down the hill, through San Anselmo, down Shady Lane until I came to the Ross School. I turned right toward Phoenix Lake and pedaled up the street past grand houses on even grander grounds, big shade trees, neatly clipped lawns, long driveways and metal gates that opened to the touch of buttons on a post nearby. When I came to Carmel Drive, I slowed, looking for 221. It had a big hedge along the front, another electron-ically- controlled metal gate, and a graveled driveway that led through an avenue of roses. I stopped, turned the bike upside down on the seat and handlebars and got out the wrench. I took off the front wheel, as if I were repairing a flat tire. No one would pay attention to a middle-aged man fixing his bike. The driveway led to a three-car garage, two stories, and Fuller had guessed right. There was a second story, which had, no doubt, at some time housed a chauf-feur. The house was big, brown shingled, some ivy clinging to it, but the trim and windows were newly painted. It was the kind of house that was a Ross classic, probably built by a banker or a real estate tycoon or perhaps somebody in the now defunct San Francisco shipping empire. It was not only big, it was substantial, and I could see an addition tacked onto one side;high glass windows, a modern conservatory of some kind. There would be a swimming pool, too, some-where on the slope behind the house. And somewhere higher up on the edge of Ross would be a lot with a horse. Three car garage. Probably a Mercedes or a Porsche and certainly something big, like a Land Rover with a full rhino package. The Ford Expedition would be gone. It was not the kind of a property where a three-year old car would be kept.

Whatever Earl Winslow did, it paid well. I took my time getting the tire off the rim, making mental notes of what I could see. There would be no point in trying to get inside that enclosure. There were, no doubt, security cameras posted. Two Hispanic men were trimming the roses, a pickup truck parked in front of the garage, the back filled with rakes, shovels, a powered lawnmower and a canvas tarp lying on the ground with clippings half filling it. They paid no attention to me. It was the middle of the day and Winslow would be at work, whatever that was. And the best way to waylay him would be when he came out of his driveway on the way to work. Which would require a few more trips to establish his routine. I needed to know where he worked, when he went to work, and it would require more observation. I needed to be the egret, waiting. I needed to see him wiggling in the mud at my feet. I needed to go back to Santa Rosa and get myself a gun. And I would stop him, and he would drive to Point Reyes and he would go into that wild surf. He would have no choice. Like my daughter, who was left no choice by Earl Winslow.

CHAPTER 7

I t didn't take much browsing on the Internet to find Earl
Winslow. CEO of a major oil company, on the board of
directors to several major corporations, a big donor to the
modern art museum; he had a high-priced box at the 49ers
stadium where he entertained an A-list of celebrities. In his
forties, a handsome man with a wife much younger than he
was, she was a real looker, prominent in photos of art open-
ings at the museum.

There were pictures of the two of them, smiling for the
camera, him in a tailored suit that fit perfectly, and she wearing a form-fitting dress that showed off her body. This was a
woman who spent time at the gym, I thought. All of which
probably meant that he didn't have a nine-to-five schedule.
But there had to be regular forays out of that fortress where
he lived. I would have to make it a routine to ride the bicycle
on Carmel Avenue. Ride up to Phoenix Lake. What I should
do was to buy myself an off-road bike, the kind that you saw
on the trails around Phoenix Lake. Buy that and a helmet
and I could make my pass around Earl Winslow's compound
a regular event, just another middle-aged man on a bike trying to reduce the flab in his legs.

I could vary the routine by parking the bike next to the
post office in Ross, locking it to the bike rack on the side-
walk, walking up to Carmel Avenue, strolling past the gate.
If I tried it at various times I was sure to spot him. Fix him
with my egret eye.

I bought the bike at the bike shop in Fairfax and began with an early morning ride. It took a week before I saw him coming out of the gate. He drove a Mercedes.

S-class, and a quick check told me it cost a hundred thousand dollars. Silver gray, it purred out of those gates, Winslow at the wheel, and he didn't give me a second glance. Ten o'clock in the morning. It took another three weeks before I was able to pin him down. Ten o'clock on Tuesdays and Thursdays, like clockwork. He had some kind of appointment on those two days. But I continued to make the rounds for another month before I was sure that this was a regular schedule. There were other departures, but they came at odd hours, often with the wife in the car as well. The wife drove a Porsche 911, yellow, and there was, as I suspected, a black Range Rover in the third bay in the garage.

So it would be a Tuesday or a Thursday.

I bought the gun from the shop in Santa Rosa. It was the Glock G43, a little over six inches long, weighing slightly more than a pound unloaded, less than a pound and a half loaded, nine millimeter, with a magazine of seven rounds. I took a class in shooting it, went to the gun range with a young man from the gun shop, put on earplugs and fired at a circular target, then at an outline of a man. I didn't do well. I imagined the target to be Winslow, and sighted carefully, but the recoil of the gun raised my aim. It took half an hour before I could hit the target.

"You'll be OK," the kid said. "Everybody has problems at first."

But I knew that I would not be raising the gun and firing at a distant figure. I would be next to him in his car, pressing the gun to his body. Missing the target didn't bother me. I was going to hold the gun to Winslow's head. It was small enough to fit in my jacket pocket and it had the look of a pistol that meant business. The gate would open and he would pause until it was fully open, then come slowly through the gate, pause before he entered the street and that was the moment. I would open the passenger door of his Mercedes and slip inside and I would press the gun to his temple and tell him to drive. And he would protest and I would jam the muzzle at his skull, hurting him, and I would lower the gun and press it into his crotch and say to him, "Drive this fucking car or I will blow off your balls and your cock," and I would press the gun more tightly against him. I wouldn't need any target practice for that.

The gun was black, had some plastic parts that contributed to its light weight, and it fit easily into my hand. I could understand how some men could become entranced with such a weapon. There was a power that was transmitted to my brain when I held the gun steady and pulled the trigger.

Now I was ready. I needed to pick a day, and it occurred to me that it would be appropriate to pick a day that corresponded to my daughter's death. The date, April 7, didn't fall on a Tuesday or a Thursday. This year it was a Wednesday, which suited me perfectly. An early April Tuesday or Thursday would mean that the North Beach at Point Reyes would be little used. With any luck, the weather would be foul, foggy, cold. Perhaps even rain. April was too soon for the summer crowds. An empty beach with a pounding surf was what I wanted. A surf that was unforgiving, that would tumble his body like a leaf in the rapids of a spring river, that would suck him down, vomit him back up and suck him down again, pressing tons of water on his helpless body. A surf that would slam him against the wet sand, break his arms and legs, leave him like a wet rag. And if the weather didn't cooperate, than I would use another day. And if he didn't appear outside his gate, I would use another day. I would remain motionless, watching his every move, waiting for the opportune moment to strike.

I had taken to looking for egrets. I saw them in the marsh behind College of Marin, alongside Highway 37 in Sonoma County, in the tidal flats, and at the edge of the bay behind the shopping mall in Corte Madera. Always, they were still. Sometimes they were solitary, a single egret standing in the marsh, waiting. Sometimes they were in pairs or more, white strokes in the green grasses, all of them still, waiting.

CHAPTER 8

I could get Winslow to drive out to North Beach. All it would take would be a gun to his head. But the problem would be how to get myself back from the beach, and leave his car there. He took a walk on the beach slipped, went into the surf, and there would be his car in the parking lot, but how would I get back to Fairfax. The answer was to get someone to come out and pick me up. I could go to the Tomales Bay Lodge, get a room, leave my car there, get someone to pick it up, drive it out to North Beach, bring me back to the lodge. Somebody who would buy the story I would tell him: that I was going to be dropped off at North Beach and needed someone to drive my car out there so I could get back. Make it sound like I was meeting someone out there that I didn't want a wife to know about. I could find somebody at the Old Western Saloon in Point Reyes. One of those guys who spent his late afternoon playing liars dice, and drinking shots and beer. Somebody who would be happy to take a drive to Inverness, get my car, go out to North Beach, bring me back to the lodge. A hundred bucks. Easy money. And he would never see me again. So what I had to do was go out to Point Reyes Station and sit in that saloon and find the right guy.

Two guys sat on my left and the one next to me had a tattoo that rose up from his collar on his neck, a complicated design. I ordered a Manhattan, rye whiskey, and he turned to me and said, "That's what I do. Rye. Only way to do it."

"Can I buy you one?"

He looked at his partner.

"Your partner, too."

"Shit, this must be our lucky day, Davy," said the partner.

"Lucky day for me, too," I said. "I've got a problem. And maybe you can solve it."

"What kind of a problem?"

"Well, I'm going to meet somebody out at North Beach. You know where that is?"

"Yeah."

"Only after I meet her, I need to get back to the Tomales Bay Lodge in Inverness. You know where that is?"

"Yeah." The bartender set the Manhattans in front of us. He had poured it to the rim and I leaned forward to sip a bit of mine before picking it up. The bartender took a glass and poured the extra Manhattan into it, set it next to my drink.

"Generous pour," I said, sliding a twenty out toward him. He rang up the drinks and put two ones in front of me. I slid them back.

"You interested?" I asked Davy, the tattooed kid.

"So you need somebody to pick you up at North Beach," he said.

"Yes. It's kind of touchy, I'd be willing to pay a hundred bucks to somebody who was willing to pick up my car at the lodge and drive it out to the parking lot at North Beach. No questions asked. Just drive it out, bring me back to the lodge and he gets a hundred bucks cash."

"How come this person you're meeting out there can't give you a ride back to Inverness?"

"It's sort of a delicate thing. I mean, it's not somebody I want to advertise. So if she brings me back and somebody sees us, then it gets sticky. Know what I mean?"

"So, you're gonna ride out there and then you need somebody to bring your car out to you?"

"That's it."

"When would this be?"

"Early in April. If I had a phone number I could make the arrangements. You interested?"

"Maybe. Is that all? Just pick up a car and drive it out to North Beach and pick you up?"

"That's it. And your discretion. You conveniently forget that you did it. You ride with me back to the lodge. "

"I've got a shitty memory."

"Drink up," I said. "There might be another one of those."

CHAPTER 9

Davy, who drives a truck for Toby's, was willing to bring my car out. A hundred bucks for what would amount to maybe two hours was good news to him. And all I have to do is set the date, lock up my bike at the Ross Post Office, walk to Carmel Drive, and wait for Winslow to come out. And if he doesn't, then I cancel Davy and we re-set it.

Detective Fuller showed up again. It was threatening rain and he wore a heavy coat, the collar turned up.

It was mid-morning.

"You don't work, do you?" he said.

"I haven't worked in three years. I paid off this house, my car is paid for, I draw some money from a 401K, and I have few expenses. I'm a carpenter. But after she died, I couldn't seem to hit the nail straight. I did shitty work. I was a finish carpenter, did quality work, and suddenly I couldn't concentrate. I left pecker tracks in the wood. Nobody likes that. Now I build birdhouses. Give them away."

"You check up on our boy, Winslow?"

"Yes. I checked up on him. He's a rich fucker. Got a trophy wife. Lives in a house that could be the lodge in a national park. "

"But you're not planning on doing anything foolish?"

"No."

"Then why did you buy a gun?"

"You checked up on me."

"That's right. Your name showed up when they ran the

security check on you. They copy the sheriff's office on all of these. Anybody in Marin County who buys a gun gets checked out by us. To see if we have them on our radar. You bought a Glock G43. Why did you suddenly decide to buy a gun?"

"No particular reason. You don't think I'm going to shoot the asshole, do you?"

"I'm not sure what it is that you're going to do. You don't live in West Oakland. There's not a rash of burglaries in your neighborhood. You don't belong to a gang. There's no longer a shooting range in Marin County. There's no rash of threats to home owners, no sudden cluster of people doing armed home entries. So why go out and buy a hand gun?"

"No particular reason. These days everybody seems to be buying a handgun. I'm no different. It's next to my bed."

"It would be a good idea if you locked it up some place. Some place where it would be difficult for you to get to it easily."

"Is this a neighborhood watch program? Does the sheriff's department do this with anybody who buys a gun?"

"No. I just don't want you to do anything foolish. Something that would put you away for the rest of your life. You shoot the sonofabitch and you'll go away for a long time, maybe the rest of your days. Guy your age, if you're lucky, they'll send you to High Desert, which is way the fuck up in the northeast corner of the state and you'll spend your time in the craft shop making birdhouses. If you're unlucky, you'll end up in San Quentin or Soledad where there are some really ugly people. You wouldn't last a month in a place like that. And it would be a month you wouldn't want to remember. Please tell me that you aren't planning on doing anything to this fuckhead."

"I'm hoping he has an accident. Maybe gets run over by a UPS truck or falls in the ocean and drowns."

"As long as you're not driving the UPS truck."

"So have you found out anything else that might connect him to my daughter's death?"

"Nothing. There's no place to look. The truck driver who saw the collision only says it was a man driving. He stopped, went down to the bay, tried to get to your daughter, but it's the deep part of the channel, just past White House Pool."

"I know where it is."

"Yeah, of course you do."

"So he gets to live out his life, no punishment, nothing?"

"Nothing I can tie to him. Maybe he feels shitty about it. Maybe he has nightmares about what happened."

"Maybe." I looked at Fuller, put my hands to my face, scrubbed my face and said, "He drives an S-class Mercedes. A hundred grand. He lives in a fucking palace. He gives a shitload of money to museums. His fucking trophy wife at his side." I could hear the rain now, drumming on the roof. Hard. The kind of day that would be a good one at North Beach. Rain driving down, the surf up, pounding on the beach, no chance for anybody who fell into that raging maelstrom.

"I tried to trace that Expedition," Fuller said. "He traded it in on a Range Rover and then it got auctioned off. Went to a dealer in Stockton. The trail gets murky there. I won't quit on this," Fuller said. "I want you to know that. If I find anything, you'll be the first one to know," he said, rising. "And lock up that fucking gun. Please."

CHAPTER 10

I had found a way to get back from North Beach. Now all I had to do was select the date, call my ride, book the lodge, and ride my bike to Ross, lock it to the bike rack at the post office, walk up to Winslow's house and climb into his car when he came out his driveway. It was perfect, as if I had waited, motionless until it was time to strike. I could see Winslow tumbling in the surf, and it felt good, as if a weight were being lifted off of me. But until he disappeared in that churning water, I would not be whole again.

Fuller reappeared. He came to my house had another scotch and told me that he had interviewed Winslow.

"He says it's a coincidence. He had nothing to do with an accident in Inverness. He scraped the car on a wall in a garage in San Francisco."

"He's a rich sonovabitch," I said

"That he is. There's no doubt about that. But I don't have anything that I can connect him to your daughter's death. That much I know."

"But you think he's the one."

"I think he's a good candidate."

"Which means you can't charge him, but you think he's the one."

"I didn't say that."

"No need to say it. I've checked out the asshole. He's richer than Midas and he had that Ford Expedition and now it's gone."

"You've been doing some research?"

"Yes. I know where he lives and I know his habits and I'm sure the sonofabitch is the one."

"Don't do anything foolish,"

"I'm not sure what foolish means. I have nothing to lose, Fuller. My daughter is dead, my wife left me, I have very little left. I no longer work as a carpenter, I can't seem to drive a nail straight, and when you show up, I think that you know something that I ought to know"

"I don't know anything that I haven't told you."

"But you know this fucker is the one, don't you?"

"I told you, he looks good for it. But I'm not positive. And I don't have any physical evidence to connect him with what happened."

"Good enough for me," I said. I poured him another scotch.

After he left I sat on the little deck looking at the mountain. What had she been doing at Hearts Desire Beach? Running into the water, swimming in that flat watered bay, drinking a beer, maybe watching someone's dog run after a tennis ball in the water, spending an afternoon with friends her age. Young people with a lifetime ahead of them, Only her lifetime was suddenly eclipsed by that passing SUV.

CHAPTER 11

I drove out to the Tomales Bay Lodge, booked a room for two nights and parked my car in front of the room. I hung the do not disturb sign on the doorknob, and put the keys to my car under a rock at the foot of the big rusted anchor that leaned against the Lodge sign at the edge of the road where Davy could find them. I walked the half-mile back into Inverness and waited in front of the grocery store for the little bus that came out to West Marin. It arrived forty-five minutes later and I boarded the bus. It stopped in Olema, again at Forest Knolls and then went over White's Hill to Fairfax where I got off. I walked back up to my house. It was Monday afternoon and tomorrow would be the day when I would stab with my beak, impale the minnow that finned at my feet, make Earl Antony Winslow pay for his carelessness.

Tuesday morning I left the bike locked to the bike stand in front of the Ross Post Office and walked to Carmel Drive. It was nine-thirty. If he were going to come out today it would be at ten. I felt in my jacket pocket for the Glock. I leaned back into his hedge on what would be the passenger side of his car when he came out. I heard the hum of the electric gate as it swung open. The car appeared, paused at the edge of the road and the gate swung shut behind it.

I strode over to the window on the passenger side and waved at him. He looked at me. I motioned to him to roll down the window.

Nice middle-aged guy, must be asking for directions. The

window rolled smoothly down. Which meant that if the door was locked I could reach in and unlock it.

"Mr. Winslow?" I said.

He nodded.

I reached for the door handle and pulled. The door was unlocked. I jerked the door open and slid in. He froze, staring at me..

"Who are you?" he said. "What the fuck is this?"

I pulled out the Glock, held it to his temple.

"Is this a carjack?" he said. "You want my car?"

"I don't want your car. I want you to drive."

"You want money? Is that what this is?"

"No. No money."

"Do I know you?"

I pressed the barrel of the gun harder into his skull. Hard enough to hurt.

"You knew my daughter. At least you had a passing acquaintance with her. It only lasted a few seconds, but it made a lasting impression on her."

"What was her name?"

"Just shut the fuck up and drive," I said. "Drive to Sir Francis Drake Boulevard, then head out toward the coast. It's a route you know well. We're going to Inverness."

"I have a house out there."

"I know, now shut up and drive." I lowered the gun and pressed it into his crotch. "If you do anything odd or anything to attract attention, I will pull the trigger and blow off your cock and balls. Is that clear? You won't be able to fuck that pretty wife of yours any more." I pressed the barrel of the gun harder into his crotch.

"What do you want?"

"Shut up and drive," I said. His knuckles were white on the steering wheel. It was the first time I had been in a hundred thousand dollar car. The ride was smooth, and there was no road noise. It was like floating in money.

We went through Fairfax, climbed over White's Hill, then threaded our way through Samuel P. Taylor State Park. He was silent, concentrating on the road and I kept the Glock pressed to his crotch. When we came to the turnoff to Inverness I said, "Turn. You know the way!" He turned onto the two-lane road and in a few minutes we were opposite White House Pool. Just beyond it, I said, "Slow down. Pull over."

He found a wide spot on the verge and brought the car to a halt.

"You recognize this spot?"

"I've been past it a hundred times. My cottage is down the road."

"No, I mean three years ago, you came around this curve on the wrong side of the road and clipped a car. Remember that?"

"No."

"Bullshit. You not only remember it, you drove off and two days later you took your car to a body shop in San Rafael to get it fixed."

"I don't remember."

"Were you so fucking drunk that you don't remember the collision, the other car in the water? The other car pinwheeled. That's the word the truck driver behind you used. Pinwheeled. And you just fucking drove away. You killed my daughter, you fucking murderer."

"I didn't do that."

"No, I'm not mistaken. You drove on and you had your

car fixed and you wrote it off, like some bad debt, some incidental thing that you could fix with a check to somebody, and then it was over for you. Write a check and everything is OK.

Money takes care of it, doesn't it? Put your pen to the checkbook and whatever happens is cancelled out. But it was not over for me, you fucking cretin. And now you're going to pay for it."

"You're going to shoot me."

"No. You're going to keep driving. You're going to drive out to North Beach on the west side of the Peninsula. The big beach side. You're going for a swim."

"You're going to shoot me and dump my body in the ocean."

"No. I'm not going to shoot you. Unless you do something stupid between now and North Beach." I pressed the gun harder into his crotch.

"Drive," I said. "Out to the end of the peninsula. Where the big beaches are. And remember that if you do anything to attract attention, swerve or drive too slow or drive erratically, I'll pull the trigger."

We passed the Tomales Bay Lodge and I could see my car in front of the room I had rented. Hopefully Davy would do what I had asked. If he didn't, I would have a long hike back from that beach, ten miles of walking, although a passing car could possibly give me a lift.

"Look," Winslow said. "I didn't sideswipe your daughter's car. You've got the wrong person."

"No, I haven't. You have a house out here. In fact, we'll pass the turnoff to it in just a moment. You had that Ford repaired two days after the accident. You paid cash for the repair and you gave a phony name and address to Gotellis. They've got a witness that says it was a Ford Expedition. A man driving it. It's you, alright."

I realized that he was speeding up. No doubt he was going to turn the car off the road, risk surviving an accident rather than take his chances with me. "Slow down," I said. "Thirty, that's the right speed for this road." I pressed the gun against his crotch harder for emphasis. We had reached the turn to the south to the big beaches, South Beach and North Beach and Drakes Beach off to the left. It would only be a few more minutes before the turnoff to North Beach. Off to the right the ocean was spread out, a low fog obscuring the horizon. It was a perfect day, cold and foggy, enough to discourage visitors. With any luck the beach would be empty. "Here," I said. "Turn here." We went down the narrow one-lane road. The road ended in the parking lot and I said, "All the way to the end." We stopped opposite the empty ranger's building. No cars other than the Mercedes.

"Leave your coat here in the front seat," I said. "When we get out, lock the car and put the keys in your pocket."

I opened the passenger door, slid out and stood, leaning back in, the gun pointed at him. "If you try to run I'll shoot you," I said.

"There must be something I can do," he said. "You've got the wrong man."

"No, I've got the right man. And there isn't anything you can do. You can't give me enough money to make up for what you did. You admit to the cops what you did and you'll get a high-priced lawyer and plead guilty to vehicular manslaughter and you'll find a way out of it. No, there's nothing you can do. Now get out."

He opened the driver's door and I moved to the front of the car, still holding the gun on him. "Now lock it. Put the keys in your pocket."

"What are you going to do?"

"We're going to take a walk on the beach."

I waved at the path with the gun. "Down there."

He moved toward the path that descended to the beach. He was wearing loafers with a silver tassel, brightly polished. My guess was that he didn't polish them himself.

He began to reach into his hip pocket but I said, "No. Keep your hands where I can see them."

"There's money in my wallet," he said "You can take the car. I can get you more money. More than you can imagine."

I pointed the gun above his head and squeezed the trigger. There was a sharp report, and he involuntarily ducked, and I said. "It works, doesn't it? You say one more word about money and I'll put a bullet in your spine. You won't be able to move, ever again."

By now we were on the soft sand just below the bluff. Ahead of us was the surf, pounding up against the sharply angled beach. The waves came in, one on top of the next, rushing madly up the sand and back into themselves. As far out as I could see, the surf was in a frenzy, the wind whipping the tops into a white mist, the faces of the waves ugly and in disarray. We had reached the edge where the white foam was at our feet. The noise of the surf was constant, the kind of noise that a subway train makes when it comes out of the tunnel, echoing, pressing against your ears. There was no way that anyone could survive more than a few seconds in that bedlam of water, a pandemonium of deadly churning.

"What you're going to do is walk into that," I said. "You

can stand here and I can shoot you and push your body into it, or you can walk into it."

"I can't survive that," he said. "Nobody can survive that."

"That's what it says on the sign up at the parking lot. The sign that says it's a dangerous beach. The sign that says people have died here." He stood there in his sharply creased suit trousers, his tasseled loafers, a white shirt with expensive jeweled cufflinks and a red tie, carefully knotted.

"You took a walk out here this morning. On a whim, you drove out here to get some fresh air and clear your head. You slipped and a sneaker wave pulled you in. And you got pulled out into that." I gestured with the pistol at the surf. "My daughter hung upside down by her seat belt and her car settled into the water and she drowned. A truck driver behind you on the road went down to try to save her. You drove off. But he couldn't do anything. Her car was upside down and it took two tow trucks to pull her car out and there she was, hanging by her seat belt, dead. Lovely girl. She wanted to be a schoolteacher. She was a swimmer, but her seat belt was jammed and the water rose and she held her breath and then the water entered her lungs and you were half a mile down the road. I wish I could put you in that fucking big car of yours and turn it upside down in the water, but I can't. So this is the next best thing. Now step into the next wave."

"You're a fucking mad man," he said.

"You got that right. I'm a fucking mad man. An angry man. Angry enough to shoot you, but that wouldn't be the way I want this to end. I want it to end with you breathing in some water. Just like she did."

He took a step closer to the water. I had the gun trained

at his midsection.

"No chance of me missing at this range," I said. "You go into that water with all your faculties working, or you go into the water with a bullet in your gut. It's your choice."

He turned to face the water and stepped out of his loafers. He was careful, as if he intended to later come back and slide his feet into them. He took several steps, and dove into the face of the next wave. It was the dive of a swimmer, someone who had taken a dive into the surf before. But this surf was wild and cold and he wouldn't last. It would tumble him and he would quickly succumb to hypothermia. His body would float ashore in a matter of hours. I watched as the next wave brought him to the surface. He was trying to swim, but the wave turned, the weight of the water pushing him down. He popped up again, this time farther out, riding the crest of another wave. I watched until he disappeared. I imagined him looking up through that transparent green, trying to get to the surface and feeling the rip tide pulling him under. North Beach was famous for its currents, which was why the sign warned people that others had died here. The next wave came up a bit farther and took his loafers, sweeping them into the sea. I watched them disappear. I looked at my watch. A half hour until Davy was scheduled to show up. I went back through the soft sand that led to the path to the parking lot. I walked past the Mercedes, until I came to where the road entered the parking lot. I waited there, the gun tucked again into my jacket pocket. This was when the egret ate its catch.

CHAPTER 12

My car came down the road, Davy at the wheel, right on time. He pulled over, opened the door.

"OK?" he said.

"Perfect," I replied. "I'll drive back to the Lodge."

He got into the passenger seat. I closed my door. "The other half," he said.

I got out my wallet and took out three twenties. "I don't have any change," I said. So it's ten extra. Which is OK." We drove back to the Lodge in silence. There was a beat-up pickup truck parked next to where my car had been.

"You'll never see me again," I said. "At least not in the Saloon. I appreciate your help."

"Not a problem," he said. "Easy money. You need me again, you know where to reach me."

"No," I said, "this is a one-off. Forget you ever met me."

He got out, climbed into his pickup and left. I opened the door to my lodge room and went in, took off my jacket and lay on the bed. I tried to imagine Winslow in the surf. This would be the last tine I would take a room at the Tomales Bay Lodge. I would no longer have to visit the spot where my daughter had died. Maybe I would even go back to carpentering. Make real houses, not birdhouses. I got up, put my jacket back on and walked out to the little marina. The tide was in and the boats floated on the shallow water. I looked out at the edge of the bay, hoping to see an egret. But there were no egrets, only seagulls and the insistent cry of crows in the trees across the road. Somewhere to the west, Winslow had drowned and now the current would take his body south until he floated onto a beach or got hung up in the rocks. Perhaps his body would sink and not surface for another week. It didn't matter. He had struggled and eventually he had breathed in the ocean just as my daughter had done. I turned on the television and found the evening news: stories of disasters in the Middle East, a fire in the Sierra foothills, but nothing about a man tumbling in the surf at Point Reyes. Perhaps another night. I napped for a while, then got up, went to the café in the lodge. I ordered the fish and chips and it came, a big plate mounded with fried fish and French fries. I had a glass of wine and I felt good. Satiated. The water in the bay outside the window was dotted with whitecaps. A good wind. The wind that had heeled that little sailboat over when my daughter had hiked out to the high side. Wind that would keep the surf up on the western side of the peninsula. A wind that would keep the surf in turmoil. I slept well that night.

CHAPTER 13

I checked out early, had breakfast at the Station House Café in Point Reyes Station. Back in Fairfax, I stopped at the corner coffee shop and had a cup of coffee, then I stopped at the 7-11 on the way home and bought a Marin Independent Journal. When I got home I looked through the paper, hoping to see an article about a man's body being found at Point Reyes, washed ashore, but there was no notice. Still too early. But the park rangers would get curious about that Mercedes, check the registration, and he would be reported as missing. Tomorrow morning's *San Francisco Chronicle* would report: TEXAS OIL CEO MISSING AT POINT REYES NATIONAL SEASHORE.

I walked to San Anselmo, had another coffee in the Roastery there and then walked on to Ross, found my bike still locked to the bike rack and rode back to Fairfax. All of the loose ends were tied up. Now the only thing left was the news that there had been another fatality on a Point Reyes Beach.

The next morning I went out to the garage, got out my carpenter's belt and laid it on the workbench. The hammer was still in its holster and there were two chisels in the pocket. They would have to be sharpened. Razor-sharp chisels were a mark of a good carpenter. My father had taught me that. He had been a cabinetmaker, a man of great precision. When I was a kid he drove me nuts, measuring things in sixty-fourths of an inch, giving me a cuff on the back of the head when I cut something on the wrong side of the pencil line. I got out a stone, oiled it and set to work sharpening one of the chisels. Today was the anniversary of my daughter's death.

I didn't hear Fuller at the door of the garage.

"Building another birdhouse?" came his voice.

I turned. "Just sharpening a chisel. I'm thinking of going back to work. Maybe work on a real house."

"What brought that on?"

"Nothing in particular. I need to do something constructive, and the birdhouses don't seem to be making it work."

"It wouldn't have anything to do with a man in the surf at Point Reyes, would it?"

My heart quickened. I continued to work the chisel against the stone. "What's that supposed to mean?" I asked.

"Somebody we both know ended up in the surf at Point Reyes yesterday," he said.

"You don't mean?" I said.

"I do mean. Winslow."

"He drowned in the surf?"

"No. He didn't. He swam parallel to the surf and a ranger at South Beach spotted him. He called the Coast Guard helicopter at Two Rock and a swimmer dropped into the water and they hauled him out. Took him to Kaiser Hospital in Santa Rosa to treat him for hypothermia. His car was still parked at North Beach."

Fuller waited. He expected a response from me.

"Holy shit. He got pulled out of the ocean? And he survived? He's the luckiest sonofabitch still living."

"You expected him to die?"

"I expect anybody who goes into that surf off one of those

beaches to die. Unless they're wearing a wet suit. And even then it's a toss-up. Was he wearing a wet suit?"

"No, he was wearing a white silk shirt with cuff links and a red tie. Not your usual garb for a walk on a beach. Especially a cold foggy morning."

"And he swam as far as South Beach?"

"The current probably did that. He was on the swim team at Santa Clara. Did you know that?"

"No, I didn't know that."

"Might have been something you ought to have known."

"You're suggesting something, Detective Fuller?"

"No, I'm not suggesting anything. But I warned you not to do anything foolish. His story is that he took a walk out there on a whim. Wanted to get some fresh air, clear his head. A sneaker wave caught him. You believe that? You believe that all on his own he drove all the way out to a Point Reyes beach so he could get some fresh air? An hour and a half. And he went for a walk on a cold foggy beach in his good clothes, all dressed up?"

I tested the blade of the chisel with my thumb, turned it and picked a sliver of wood off the edge of the workbench. It was sharp enough.

"Why wouldn't I believe it?"

"Because it's improbable. He has an eleven o'clock appointment in his offices every Tuesday and Thursday. Important meeting. Never misses it. Only Tuesday he drove all the way out to North Beach, parked his car, locked it, and fell into the ocean. Wearing the trousers to a suit that cost a thousand bucks and cuff links that cost more than your little Toyota. He insists that his story is true. Stupid idea, he said."

"You talked to him?"

"No. The National Park Rangers did. Only his story showed up on the morning sheriff's log, which I look at out of curiosity, and I talked to the deputy who made our call. He talked to the ranger that spotted him. The ranger said he was checking the South Beach parking lot because they had some hippies who had built a fire there Sunday night and he wanted to make sure they had moved on and then he saw something out beyond the surf line that didn't look like a sea lion; there seemed to be an arm waving and then it disappeared, so he got out his glasses and there was Winslow, obviously in trouble, so he called the Coast Guard and they scrambled a helicopter and twenty minutes later they had Winslow in the air. The ranger is pretty stoked about the rescue. Which he ought to be. So what do you think?"

"I think it would have been good if the ranger had looked the other way. That's what I think."

"You got any ideas about how Winslow ended up in the surf?"

"No."

"But if you had anything to do with it, Winslow would know what you look like, right?"

"Why would he know that? He's never seen me."

Fuller leaned against the side of the open garage door. "Let's see," he said. "This is, of course, hypothetical, but if, somehow, somebody managed to force Winslow out to that beach, force him into the water, then Winslow would know what that person looks like. And Winslow doesn't say anything because that person connected him to another crime, committed several years ago. So what Winslow wants to do is find that guy and silence him. Which means that the guy, the fictional guy, you understand, is now in danger of a rich man who can hire all the thugs he wants, looking for him. And when he finds him, who knows what he's gonna do? Of course, that's all hypothetical."

"Why are you telling me this?"

"Because you're not stupid. But you did a stupid thing. Eventually Winslow is going to connect you to his morning swim. And he's going to want to deal with you. I don't know what else to say. You need to watch your back. You need to learn to use that Glock that you bought. I doubt if you'll ever get close to him again. I feel your pain. I sympathize with you. No, that's not the right word. I empathize with you. He's the luckiest sonofabitch in the world. He ought to be washing up on a beach about now, but he isn't. He's in that fucking big house of his and he's probably making some phone calls. He's a prick and you have every right to hate his guts, but there's no point in you getting hurt just because he's a world class prick. That's all I've got to say."

"You want a scotch?"

"Too early in the day for me."

"You want a bird house?" I pointed to a row of birdhouses on a shelf at the end of the garage.

"No. I'm not big on birds."

He shifted his weight from the edge of the door. "You be careful," he said. "I'm not going to tell you not to do anything stupid. You won't pay attention to me. You didn't the last time I said it."

"Thanks for stopping by."

"He's alive. Which means that you're not facing a murder investigation. You and I both know what you've done. I don't know the details, but he didn't take a walk on the beach by himself. Go back to pounding nails. Keep your nose clean. I'm not cutting you any more slack."

He turned toward the open garage door, then turned to look back at me.

"I hope I've made myself clear."

"You have," I said

He nodded, turned and walked back up the driveway to his car.

I went back into the house. I poured myself a scotch and took it to the small deck in the back where I could look at the mountain. The house behind me was filled with things that brought to the surface the memory of my wife and daughter; somehow, I had been unable to clear them out. There were the little vases that my daughter had done in ceramics class in high school, delicate things that suggested she had a talent for ceramics. But when the class ended, so did the vases. There was a photograph I took of her against the posters in her room, a black and white photograph that showcased the rock concerts she had attended. It was pinned to the door of the room where she had slept There was no picture of my wife. She left without taking anything, no pictures, no silverware, nothing, She packed a bag and she was gone and it was as if she had never been there. I realized that there wasn't much left that was hers. Everything had been ours, the dishes and the pictures on the walls and the furniture that we had bought, but there was nothing that was stamped with her name.

But my daughter was there. She hovered over everything. She was a presence in the house, always there, a shadow at my shoulder when I cooked dinner and now on the deck, I could feel her presence. A hummingbird came to the feeder that hung at the edge and I watched it, an iridescent thing, so tiny that it beggared imagination, and its heart had to weigh less than a postage stamp, but it hovered at the feeder, taking the sugared water, its wings a blur and I thought, perhaps that's my daughter, reincarnated as something she admired, only I knew that it wasn't her. She was dead. Drowned in the rising water.

CHAPTER **14**

It was Davy at the door and there was his old truck parked at the top of the driveway.

"Surprised to see me?" he asked.

"Not particularly." But I was surprised to see him. There he stood, the tattoo at the side of his neck coming up out of his shirt, wearing jeans worn at the knees, workboots and a grin.

"You weren't hard to find," he said.

"And why did you want to find me?"

"Maybe it would be better if we talked inside."

"Why? Your truck is parked out front. What have you got to say?"

"I think that hundred bucks you gave me isn't enough."

"You drove my fucking car ten miles. It took you a couple of hours of your time. Seems pretty good pay to me."

"You think I'm some dumb shit-kicker who can be bought for a few bucks. You think I can't add two and two. Well, you need to wise up. Some guy got picked up out of the surf the same day you had me pick you up. There was a big Mercedes at the far end of the parking lot and it turned out to be his. And there was nobody else on that beach that I could see. So I'm guessing that you had something to do with that poor sucker ending up in the drink. At least I don't think you want me to go to the sheriff and tell him about picking up your car and driving out to North Beach just about the time that sucker took his bath. Am I right?"

"I don't know what the fuck you're talking about."

"A ranger comes into the saloon and he tells us about some rich dude who got picked up out of the surf at South Beach, and his car was at North Beach and he was wearing his good clothes, and there you were at North Beach without your car, so I put two and two together. I may not be a whiz at math but I can put two and two together. So I figure that you'd like me to keep this to myself. That was what you said to me. You said you'd like me to forget I ever met you. Forget I drove your car for you, and I figure it's worth a lot more than a hundred bucks for me to keep my mouth shut"

"I don't know what the fuck you're talking about."

"Yes, you do. And I'm thinking that there ought to be at least another zero on what you gave me. And maybe a three instead of a one at the front of it."

"You want me to pay you three thousands bucks for this shit? In case the ranger didn't tell you, that rich dude told him that he went out for a drive and got caught by a sneaker wave and got swept out. He said it was stupid of him, and he didn't say anything about anyone else. "

"And how do you know this?"

"I've got a friend who's with the sheriff's office. He read the report."

"And why would he tell you?"

I had slipped up. And this hayseed truck driver was no hayseed.

"Because I was out there at that Lodge when it happened and I saw the report in the paper and I asked him about it. I've been out to North Beach. It's fucking dangerous, and people have been pulled into that surf and died. I used to go out there with my wife and daughter."

"And all that bullshit about me bringing your car out because you needed to get back and you didn't want somebody to see you with some person. Somebody who wasn't around when I picked you up?"

"Look. I asked you to do something for me. I asked you to bring my car out there. I have no idea what happened to some rich bastard who got himself in trouble. And there's no way that I'm going to pay you three thousand dollars. It's not worth it to me."

He reached down to scratch his knee through his jeans. When he stood again he was still grinning. "I think you'll think this over," he said. "And I think you'll decide that I'm worth it. I think you'll figure out that I'm worth listening to. A sheriff's deputy comes in to the saloon when he's off duty. He knows everybody in there. He knows me. He knows I'm not a bullshitter. I went to the Lodge and I asked BJ, who works at the desk in the afternoons, about the guy in room 19. The guy with the Toyota. And he said he hadn't seen him all day. But he had the room for another night. And I said, I met you in the saloon and you left your phone on the bar and I had your phone and I wanted to return it to you, and you said you were staying out at the lodge and. I figured you'd give me a reward, and BJ said, that was likely, and he gave me your address. So here I am. And if a simple shit-kicker like me can find you, somebody else can. "

"Get the fuck out of my sight. You want to tell the sheriff some story about me getting you to drive my car out there, that's OK with me. If push comes to shove, I can produce the person who drove me out there, and you'll have shit on your face."

He continued to grin. "No, I think you'll think this over. You have my number. It's the one you called to set up the car pickup. I'm not greedy. Three thousand bucks means I can get a new truck. Nothing fancy, but something that's more dependable than what I have. Nobody else knows that I know you. Nobody. I didn't tell anybody at the bar and our hundred-dollar deal is between you and me. And the three thousand will be between you and me. Nobody else. I can keep my mouth shut. Think about it. But don't think too long." He turned and walked back up to his truck.

I watched him, waited until he fired up the engine, backed out into the street. He was something else that was loose. Something I hadn't counted on. I thought of the Glock. I could kill him, put a bullet into him and it would be another West Marin mystery, a senseless killing that couldn't be connected to a retired carpenter in Fairfax. Nobody else knows, he had said. Nobody to connect him with me. I can keep my mouth shut, he had said. Which meant that nobody knew he had come to me, nobody knew he had parked his truck in my driveway and tried to suck more money out of me. Nobody else knew. I could just wait for him until he took his truck of hay into Petaluma, and wait for him to come to a stop sign and pop him. Plenty of empty space in West Marin. The three thousand he wanted would turn into another three thousand and five thousand and ten thousand. He wouldn't stop. I could see him sitting next to me at the bar, the tattoo rising from his shirt collar, green and red lines in an intricate design, part of what looked like a dragon. I remembered him banging the cup on the bar, calling out "six fives," and his partner turning over his cup and saying "shit!" and a dollar bill sliding between them. Playing liars dice for a buck. No, he wouldn't be satisfied with three thousand. He was a loose cannon and he would slide across the deck and slam into the railing. I needed to pitch this loose cannon overboard. I had pressed that gun into Winslow's crotch and now I wished I had pulled the trigger. Davy's grinning face stayed with me, and I knew that it would be easy to stop his grinning face, put him out of the way, make it possible for me to finish my business with Winslow. I would turn my attention to Winslow. The young truck driver hadn't counted on my new identity: I was the egret, waiting to strike, and he was a minnow, finning in the shallows at my feet.

CHAPTER 15

The next day I drove out to Point Reyes Station, arriving just as the Bovine Bakery opened at six thirty. I parked on the back street near the public toilets where I could get a good look at the lumber yard and the parked trucks at Toby's Barn. I watched as Davy came out of the Bovine Bakery with a bag of goodies and a paper cup of coffee. He crossed to the yard, went to a truck tractor and opened the door., and I knew what he would do. He would drive it out, hook up to the load of hay somewhere not far from the yard and drive the load into Petaluma or Santa Rosa, or even farther north, Healdsburg or Cloverdale. The diesel engine fired up, a black cloud belching from the pipes, and then the motor settled into a low rumble. I waited until he pulled out of the yard onto Highway One, the main street that ran through the town. He turned left, which meant that he was headed for Stinson Beach and the ranches that were between Olema and Stinson. I drove to the end of the street and looked down towards the highway, saw the cab of the big truck appear and then turn and I followed. I stayed well behind him. There was no difficulty following him since the road ran in only one direction, a turnoff at Olema that he didn't take and then the long stretch to Stinson.

Near Five Brooks he turned into a field where the trailer was waiting, loaded with hay bales. I stopped the car, watched while he backed into the loaded trailer, the trailer sliding onto the hitch at the back of the tractor cab. He locked things into place, hooked up the air hoses and climbed back into the cab. He eased forward toward the gate and I drove into the slot, blocking his progress. I waved my hand out the window. His hand came out and he waved back. Obviously he thought I had come with the money. Here I was, and it was payday for him. I got out of the car, walked over to the idling truck. I stepped up onto the running board, leaned in the open window on the passenger side.

"How'd you know I was here?" he said. Those were his last words. I pulled the Glock out of my jacket pocket, aimed it at his head and pulled the trigger. His head slammed against the window on his side and the window shattered.

It was easy. It was like using a nail gun. Bang bang bang, sixteen penny nails into a stud, driven to their heads, cleaner than a hammer. Pick up the nail gun, aim it, press the trigger, and there was a three inch nail driven all the way to the head, modern technology, no longer holding that nail with your fingers, holding the hammer, striking the nail, sometimes missing, sometimes striking our own thumb, sometimes bending the nail, forcing you to pull it out and start over. Now it was just press the trigger and it was done. And I had pulled the trigger and Davy was done, slumped against the shattered window on his side of the cab, blood everywhere, the diesel engine still running. I backed off, turned, went to my car. Behind me, the truck continued to idle and when I drove away I didn't feel differently. I didn't feel any sort of remorse, not what I thought I would feel. All I could think of was that Davy was silenced, and now I could concentrate on Winslow. Davy had been greedy. Davy had tried to step beyond his limits and I had struck, my sharp bill descending through the water with unerring accuracy, spearing his body. Swallowing him. This time Winslow would die and this time I would make sure that he didn't escape.

CHAPTER **16**

The news of Davy's death was a front page article in the Independent Journal. WEST MARIN MAN KILLED AT WORK. The article told of the Sheriff's deputies being called by a rancher who found Davy's truck sitting in the field, out of fuel. Inside was Davy's body and the Sheriff's deputy told the reporter that there was no evidence of anyone else at the scene, just the truck, loaded and ready to be driven from the field, and the driver shot inside the cab. Investigation was ongoing, the article said. There was the hint that it was a drug deal gone wrong.

Nothing else. Nobody came to call on me. I cleaned the Glock, locked it in a cupboard in the garage. I spent several days cleaning up my tools and then I called Ken Kowalski, a contractor I had worked for in the past.

"I'm looking for work," I said.

"I thought you retired. At least that was the word at the union hall."

"No, I took some time off. Maybe you heard about my daughter's death. It took the starch out of me, but things have settled down, and if you're interested, I'm available."

"Of course I'm interested. These days it's hard to find somebody who knows which end of the hammer to hold onto. I've got a job in Ross going right now."

"Not Ross," I said. "I'd prefer something a bit farther away from home."

"Suit yourself," he said. "How about Petaluma? I've got a

kitchen remodel going and I need somebody to do cabinets."

"Just my thing," I said.

So I went to the job in Petaluma, spent several days tearing out old cabinets and installing new ones. The work was familiar and Ken was happy with what I did. And while I was tearing the old cabinets off the wall and installing new sheetrock and hanging the new cabinets, I thought about Earl Winslow. I thought about how he had dived into the face of that wave. That should have been a clue for me. I should have shot him right there. But of course that would have led to a police investigation when they recovered a body with a gunshot wound. If they recovered it. Still, there had to be some other way to deal with him. I watched him dive into that wave again and again. Every time I ripped a nail out of the wall or peeled off part of cabinet, I saw him stepping out of his loafers, running toward the water, suddenly head down, arms outstretched, cleaving into that wild water, like somebody who had experience swimming in the sea. He had been lucky. He had swum parallel to the breaker line, knowing that he couldn't get back in where I was, but looking for a break in the surf and three miles south he got lucky. A ranger, a thousand to one chance looks out, says to himself, hey, there's a sea lion. Whoops! What's that? An arm. Let me get my glasses out of the truck. Holy shit, it's a man out there, and he's in trouble. What the fuck is he doing out there? The helicopter at Two Rock plucks somebody off a rock or a cliff or out of a drifting boat several times a year He didn't even lose his fucking cuff links! Only he's a fucking seashore incident, another person who foolishly waded too close to that dangerous surf. Another statistic.

Detective Fuller showed up again.

"You're off somewhere during the day," he said.

"I'm back at work."

"Good idea. Idle hands are the devil's playground."

"That's nice. I should remember that."

"Our friend Winslow has changed his habits."

"Why should I be interested?"

"Probably no particular reason. And then, again, it might be something that would pique your interest. He no longer drives his car himself. He has a driver. An ex-cop who's carrying a weapon."

"And how do you know this?"

"Because I stopped by, asked him about his dip in the ocean, said we were following up on his accident. I told him the Sheriff was concerned that nothing untoward would happen to him. He said he was pleased that we were concerned, but he had done something stupid, got punished for it by the ocean, and was lucky to survive. He said he was making a generous donation to the Coast Guard fund for the relatives of officers who had lost their lives in rescue attempts. I asked him about his car, the one we found in the parking lot at North Beach. Was he still driving it? Just routine, I said. And he said, no, he had a driver, gave me his name. So I ran a check on the guy and he came up with a permit to carry. He was a cop in Oakland who retired. Apparently he now lives in the quarters over Winslow's garage."

"Why would I give a shit about this?"

"No particular reason."

"So this is just a social call?"

"You could call it that. You mind telling me where you were last Wednesday morning?"

"Probably right here. I didn't go back to work until Friday. Why?"

"Nothing much. I'm working another case, kid who got bushwhacked out at Five Brooks. A nine millimeter. Isn't that what you bought?"

"You think I shot some kid out in West Marin?"

"No. I didn't say that. You still got that gun you bought?"

"I did what you told me to do. I locked it up where I can't easily get to it."

"That's good."

"And I have no interest in Earl Winslow. That's water under the bridge." And I suddenly had an image of water and my daughter hanging upside down in it.

"I appreciate your efforts, but unless you can come to me and say, I've got the goods on that sonovabitch and we're going to trial and we're going to put him away for the rest of his life, then I'm no longer interested in anything about him. I hope that's clear."

"I'm glad to hear you say that."

We talked a bit about the shut-down of the Johnson Oyster Farm at Drake's Bay. He said he thought it was bullshit, that the National Park was riding roughshod over the owner's rights. I agreed with him. Actually, I didn't care one way or another, was only vaguely aware of the controversy. And then he left.

Why had he asked me about my Glock? Had he talked to somebody who had talked to Davy? Had he come across my stay at the Tomales Bay Lodge? Had he talked to the clerk who had given Davy my address? Had the bartender at the Old Western remembered me talking to Davy? But he had left with the comment, "I'm glad to hear you say that." Apparently Fuller was leaving me alone, had come to warn me that Winslow now had an armed driver protecting him. I would have to be more careful.

THE SNAKE

CHAPTER **17**

It was an old article from the weekly West Marin newspaper, *The Point Reyes Light.* I had gone on-line to see if there was more about the death of David Lansdale, a truck driver from Point Reyes Station. And then, while browsing back issues, I came across the article about the old Synanon headquarters on Tomales Bay. There had been bad blood between the Synanon residents, a hippie group that practiced a drug rehab program without doctors and was apparently involved in practices that involved holding children against their will. And the adjoining rancher had accused them of encroaching on his land, and of violating their use permit. So they put a rattlesnake into his mail box at the edge of the road with its rattle cut off. But the plot failed. The Point Reyes Light ferreted out the details, and there were letters and notes that helped to incriminate the Synanon head. The Point Reyes Light got the Pulitzer Prize for reporting on the Synanon story, beating out major newspapers like the *New York Times* and the *Washington Post.* A little weekly newspaper had won journalism's most sought-after prize. But that wasn't what interested me. What interested me was the fact that the houses on the streets of Ross all had street-side mailboxes. Some were old-fashioned metal boxes, others were fancy designer boxes, but they all collected their mail from the side of the street. And the rattlesnake in the mailbox lit up for me. And it was now May and rattlesnakes were no longer dormant. Somebody at Winslow's house would go out to his mailbox to get the mail. Because the houses were all separated from the streets by gates and hedges, there were mailboxes on posts. The mailmen drove up in little trucks with right-hand drive, leaned out and stuck the mail into the box. So after the mailman left, a rattlesnake inserted into the box would be waiting for whoever came for that day's mail. It was possible, of course, that a house worker would be dispatched for the mail. Or it could be the wife. Or Winslow when he came home. The car might pause, Winslow would get out and get the mail. Or, he might ask the driver to do it. It would require more observation sessions. Find out when the mailman delivered. Find out who picked up the mail from the mailbox and when. Finding a rattlesnake wouldn't be difficult. There were lots of them up around Lake Lagunitas and Bon Tempe Lake above Fairfax. Or up on the ridge above my house, near Tamarancho, the Boy Scout Camp. They could be found among rocks, in piles of old wood, and now that the days were getting warmer, they would be out in the early morning, using the warmth of paths or meadows to warm their bodies.

While it was not a foolproof scheme, it would be enough to cause Winslow serious pain. And it would remind him that there was someone out to do him harm. Keep him on edge. Make him uncomfortable. And he would want to find me. Which shouldn't be all that difficult. Davy had found me. He would, no doubt, send someone to take care of me. Perhaps that new driver of his. Or he would hire someone. Finding me and eliminating me would consume him, just as his actions had consumed me. And in trying to erase my threat, he would have to do things that would expose him to discovery. He would be the one moving. I would remain still, like the egret. Wait.

So I checked with the Ross Post Office about mail deliveries, found out that the mail trucks all came from San Anselmo. A call to San Anselmo told me that the carrier on Carmel Drive didn't get there until late afternoon. Depends on the mail, the supervisor said. Four o'clock, maybe later if there's a heavy volume.

I began to work half days for Ken, spending my afternoons on my bicycle touring the avenues of Ross. I wore a helmet that obscured my head and face, and let my beard grow so that all anyone could see of me was the brush of beard inside the bicycle helmet.

It didn't take long to get the mailman's schedule. And it didn't take long to find out that most days the wife came down to the mailbox to get the mail. But on Tuesdays and Thursdays, Winslow came back from wherever he went on those days and the car paused at the gate. The gate was activated, swung open, and the driver drove close enough to the mailbox so that Winslow could reach out from his place in the back seat and take whatever mail was in there. Then the car went forward, the gate closed and the car disappeared inside the garage.

So I spent my late afternoons up at Lake Lagunitas and Bon Tempe, poking in rock piles with a dead branch, and sure enough, I found a rattler. I had made a snake catcher, a long stick with a screw eye at the end and a short length of cord running through it. Looping the cord around the rattlesnake just behind its head, I pulled on the cord, tightening it, cinching the rattlesnake to the end of the stick, and then it was a simple matter to put the snake into a heavy jute bag. I kept the snake in the garage in a box, and, using the snake stick, held the snake so I could cut off the rattles. The tail still vibrated, but the buzzing of the rattle was gone.

I lashed a box to the back of my bike and on a Tuesday, put the rattler into the jute bag and placed it into the box and took off for Ross. I waited at the top of the street until the mailman had deposited the mail in Winslow's box, then rode down, paused at the box, leaned my bike into the hedge and brought the jute bag out of the box. I put the opening of the bag into the mailbox and shook the bag, I could feel the snake moving and when I was sure it was inside the mailbox, I lifted the door until it was nearly closed, withdrawing the empty bag. Now the snake was inside, with the mail. I rode back to Fairfax, thinking of that creature waiting, coiled up and then the hand reaching inside and the sudden strike. And when he withdrew his hand, the snake's fangs would still be sunk into his skin and the sight of the snake would bring a shriek from him. His hand would swell, and if what I had found on the internet was accurate, his hand would become the size of a softball, the skin stretched and hard, turn blue, he would have to get anti-venom shots and then his wrist and arm would swell. The snake's venom breaks down tissues so the injury would be painful and would last for weeks. He would not die. Very few people died from rattlesnake bites. But the results were devastatingly painful and long-lasting.

I went down to Fradalizio's Italian restaurant and had a celebratory dinner. The old waiter brought me a glass of Italian red wine and made a generous pour. I had been in that restaurant many times with my wife and daughter. I had the halibut, poached and served with sautéed vegetables and afterwards I went up the street to Nave's bar and had a scotch and watched the baseball game on the television hanging above the bar. I imagined Earl Winslow in the emergency room at Marin General Hospital, filled with painkillers, his wrist and arm swelling and turning blue.

CHAPTER 18

Two days later the Independent Journal had the story. ROSS MAN BITTEN BY RATTLESNAKE IN MAILBOX. The reporter even made reference to the thirty-year old Synanon story. There wasn't much there. A rattlesnake with its rattle cut off had been placed in the mailbox of the CEO of Texas Oil. Police were checking to see if disgruntled shareholders might be responsible, but the victim, Earl Winslow, discounted that theory. "It's somebody who bears me a grudge," he was quoted. "I have no idea who it might be. Maybe a shareholder, somebody who lost some money and blames me. But those kinds of people don't put rattlesnakes into mailboxes. They go after the money. This has to be somebody with a personal vendetta. And I haven't a clue who it could be. This could have been my wife sticking her hand into that mailbox or one of the maids."

But, of course, he did know who it might be. It would be the man who held a gun to his crotch and forced him to dive into the surf at North Beach. The man who believed that he had clipped his daughter's car and sent her pinwheeling into Tomales Bay where she drowned. The man who knew that he had driven away from that accident and had covered his tracks.

So the snake had bitten him and he was in pain. That much felt good. Now he would seek me out, try to put an end to me. I would have to be on the lookout for his next move. And Fuller was right. I needed to get the Glock out and practice with it. Become familiar with its workings, carry it with my tools when I went to work. Have it by my bedside when I slept.

I was not surprised to get another visit from Detective Fuller.

"You've been busy," he said, standing in my garage doorway while I unloaded my tools from my car.

"The job in Petaluma is almost finished. Not sure where I'll be next week."

"I was thinking of something besides carpentering." He said.

"And what would that be?"

"Our mutual friend, Mister Winslow, got some mail that was apparently addressed to him and it caused him a great deal of pain."

"You mean the snake in his mailbox? I read about it in the paper."

"My guess is that you did more than read about it."

"You think I put that snake in there?"

"Your fingerprints were not on his mailbox. Whoever did it must have worn gloves." He pointed at my work gloves. "Those would be good. Leather, good for handling a dangerous reptile."

"Is Winslow accusing me of doing it?"

"No, he's not accusing anyone. Which is why I stopped by. I don't think you'll get a snake in your mailbox. I think you'll get something much more deadly."

"Why aren't you charging me with a crime? If you think you know so much, why aren't you putting the cuffs on me? Because I had nothing to do with Winslow's problems. Somebody else is fucking with him. A man like that probably has more enemies than you can count. You come around here and you drop little hints that I'm the one who put him in the ocean, I'm the one who put a snake in his mailbox, and it's beginning to get on my nerves. You said you empathize with me. OK, you empathize with me. But you keep telling me I've done stupid things and you keep hinting that I'm the person responsible for that asshole's difficulties, and like I told you, I'm done with him. I'm back at work, I've got a life to live and I can live it whether he gets bitten by a snake or not."

"You still have that Glock you bought?"

"Why do you ask?"

"Because the case I'm investigating, the kid who got whacked out at Five Brooks got whacked by a nine mil. And you bought a nine mil. And this kid was killed in West Marin and that's where Winslow took his near-fatal swim. And I'm just wondering. That kid was a truck driver who spent a lot of time on those roads out there. Did he see something that he wasn't supposed to see? I don't think you're capable of doing something like that, but I've got a spent bullet from the kid's head and I'd just like to rule out any connection you might have."

"Are you fucking crazy? You think I could go out there and shoot some kid? A kid who is probably the same age as my daughter was?"

"What makes you say that? You know how old he was?"

"You keep calling him a kid."

"So, you still have the Glock?"

"As a mater of fact, I don't. I put it out here in the garage. You said to put it somewhere that I couldn't get to it easily, so I put it in a cupboard out here and somebody broke in and stole some tools and they took the gun too."

"You reported it missing?"

"Not yet. I've been busy. And frankly, I was just as glad that it was gone. I had no business buying that thing."

Fuller shifted his weight.

"So you're telling me that the gun was stolen this past week?"

"Yes."

"I get uneasy when I ask somebody about their gun and they tell me that their gun was stolen or lost. What I don't want to think is that you had anything to do with that kid's death. But two things weigh on me: that swim Winslow took and that rattlesnake in his mailbox. I know how you feel about him. I find it hard to believe that you've simply wiped him off your slate. The fact that you're back at work is a good sign. File a report on your missing gun with the Fairfax cops. File a report on the theft of your tools. I'll repeat myself. Don't do anything foolish or stupid. Mind your own business. And if anybody threatens you, let the cops know. Let me know."

He continued to lean on the edge of the garage door.

"You finished here?" I asked.

"I hope so. I hope I'm finished." He left.

CHAPTER 19

If I got rid of the Glock, threw it into the bay or buried it, then I would have nothing to defend myself if Winslow sent somebody after me. But keeping it was a risk. Obviously it wouldn't take much to match the slug they had from the kid's death and my gun. And Fuller was sniffing around. Would he talk to the clerk at the Tomales Bay Lodge? Of course he would. And the bartender at the Old Western might remember me talking to Davy. Would Davy's partner at the bar remember the guy who bought them Manhattans?

I wondered what creatures preyed on the egrets. I found out that raccoons and rats raided nests for the chicks, but the adults had little to fear. The occasional coyote might attack while an egret was foraging in a field, and hawks were another danger, but egrets wading in a marsh or at the edge of a bay had little to fear. Such a big bird with a long, dangerous beak was not something to mess with.

My house is small, what used to be a summer cottage for a San Francisco family, a place out of the fog to go to when it got hot in Marin. A place for the family to bathe in the summer sun, raise tomatoes in a small garden, the father going to and from work in the city on the ferry, the children running in the grassy hills above the cottage. Built as a summer cottage, it had been remodeled over the years, utilities brought up to date, the kitchen pulled out, new appliances and cupboards installed, and I had done much of that work myself. It was still small, two bedrooms, a kitchen, a living room and a covered porch across the back that looked out toward Mt. Tamalpais. Trees on all sides, there was a steep driveway that climbed to the narrow street, a small garage that might have been used years ago to house a small car, a Model T or a Model A, but not large enough for my Toyota. I installed a workbench where I keep my chop saw, cupboards and shelves for other tools. I'm on a slope so that the back of the house is on stilts, the front at ground level. The bedroom I choose has a view of the mountain. It's a quiet neighborhood, the occasional dog barking at a deer that wanders through, and sometimes, in the early morning, I can hear the high-pitched howl and trill of coyotes on the ridge above my street. At night the only sound is the occasional owl, a far-off dog bark, and the sound of an automobile, somebody coming home late. Otherwise, it's a silent neighborhood, which is why, when I heard the scratching, I awoke. Was it a raccoon trying to get at the garbage can? A rat chewing on a shingle on the side of the house? No, it was something at the front door, something working at the latch. I reached out to where the Glock was positioned on the bedside table. I slipped out of bed, crossed the living room to the front door. The handle was turning, and there was something being inserted between the jamb and the door. Someone was trying to get into my house.

"Keep doing that," I said, "and I will put a bullet through this door." The scratching stopped, the doorknob stilled.

"You're not fucking around with somebody who's easy pickings," I said. I went to the window and looked out into the darkness. I could see a shape, briefly illuminated by the street light at the top of the driveway. Winslow had sent someone and whoever it was now knew that I was alert at night.

Fuller had been right. Winslow would try something else. I would install motion-sensitive lights outside the house so that if anyone else showed up, the outside would immediately be lit up. I would carry the Glock with me in my tool box. And I would figure out something that would make Winslow think twice before trying again. I would make his life miserable. Make him look over his shoulder every time he left his fortress of a house. Make him surround himself with armed men. I would find something that was more deadly than a rattlesnake.

I went back to bed. I lay there in the dark, waiting. Waiting for what? I thought. Be still, I told myself. Be as still as an egret, waiting at the tide line, waiting in the mud at the edge of Tomales Bay, waiting in the marsh behind the shopping center, waiting for something to move. Winslow had moved. Now I needed to fix him with my eye, strike when it was time. The sky outside the window began to grow light, the top of Mt. Tamalpais grew distinct. This was the room my daughter had slept in. She, too, had watched the sun grow on the mountain. If she were alive today, she would be entering her senior year at university, She would have taken courses for her teaching credential. She wanted to be an elementary school teacher, and I could imagine her in a classroom, surrounded by eager children who did not reach up to her waist. She would have been good at it. Again, the image of her submerged in water filled my head. She was upside down and the water was green and shimmered and it enveloped her. Fish swam in front of me, and things floated up into the water from the floor of the car, a paper coffee cup, a receipt from the burger shop in town, tissues and one of a pair of old flip flops, the kind she wore at the beach. It all floated between me and her face and then it stopped, a rush of water and air ballooning as the car was lifted and now I was on the highway as the water rushed from the open car doors. It was the same dream every time. It was four o'clock, the light just beginning to grow and today I would go to a new job in Santa Rosa, another kitchen, more cabinets. Ken was happy with my work, and the cabinets came from IKEA, were pre-fitted, easy to install. All I had to do was replace the kitchen wall, hang the cabinets, make sure they worked properly. Two days at the most. A house at the end of a cul-de-sac, not an easy place for someone to sneak into. I would be safe today and tomorrow.

THE BOMB

CHAPTER 20

The evening news was on and there was a report on Iraq. The reporter stood amid the wreckage of a street, houses in rubble, and in front of him was the shattered remains of an army HumVee.

"Here is where they met their death," he said, gesturing toward the wreckage.

"They drove over an IED, an improvised explosive device, and it blew up under the vehicle, sending it into the air. Inside, the four men were trapped. Two of them are in the field hospital, bound for care in a German facility where they will be prepped for artificial limbs, and the other two were blown to pieces by this device." He held up some fragments of metal.

"This is all that's left," he said, holding up a piece of the bomb.

Suddenly it dawned on me. Men in that foreign country had figured out a way to blow up soldiers who drove armored vehicles. Winslow drove an expensive Mercedes, but it wasn't armored. And if they could figure out a way to blow up soldiers, then I could figure out a way to blow up Earl Anthony Winslow.

I watched the rest of the report carefully. But there was nothing about how the bomb was constructed, only details about the number of such weapons. Apparently at the beginning of that war soldiers were killed by rifle fire or mortar attacks but now the majority of the injuries came from these bombs, placed where vehicles traveled, set off by re-mote control, using simple mobile phones as the trigger-ing device. If terrorists in a foreign country under siege by another army, denied the usual avenues to materials, could make such weapons, how complicated could they be?

I went to my computer and googled IEDs. What I found was that the idea went back to the 1960's when members of the Irish Republican Army fashioned bombs to blow up British soldiers and pubs frequented by the opposition. The bombs had gotten more sophisticated, but the principle re-mained the same. Make an explosive device, figure out a way to detonate it from a distance, often not far away and when the vehicle filled with soldiers drove over it, boom! It shattered their lives.

I could imagine Winslow's expensive Mercedes driving out of his gate, turning onto Carmel Drive and suddenly there was an explosion, a crater in the street and the car would be on its side, shattered, and Winslow would be ei-ther dead or in pieces, requiring a pain-filled rehabilitation, dealing with replacement limbs and possibly a damaged brain, rendering him *non compos mentis*. It would be the per-fect way to deal with the fucker.

CHAPTER 21

I went for a walk around the block. I met a neighbor who was walking his dog and I stopped to pet it. It had three legs.

"I got it from the Humane Society," he said. "Nobody wanted the little fucker and he's as good on three legs as any dog on four." The dog was small and black and shy. I remembered a dog that a cousin of mine had, a three legged dog named Skippy. The cousin lived on a farm. When they mowed a field, the pheasants and rabbits gathered in the unmowed center, and then the dogs rushed in, flushed them and the farmers, who had brought their shotguns, downed the birds. But Skippy rushed in too soon, got his leg cut off by the mower that hadn't shut down yet. He recovered, and was as lively as this dog in front of me. "What's his name?" I asked.

"Bailey."

"You're doing OK, Bailey," I said as I scratched his ears. A dog with three legs doesn't need an artificial leg . It hops about as if it were born with three legs. But Winslow wouldn't be able to hop about. If he lost a leg it would require months of rehabilitation and an artificial leg, something he would have to unbuckle every night. I scratched Bailey's ears once again

"You're doing OK, Bailey," I said. The rest of the walk was the usual, crows croaking from the trees above me, the light filtering through the trees. I thought about Skippy, my cousin's dog. He had been a dog that was fiercely protective of the house and outbuildings. Anybody who showed up uninvited risked that three-legged dog's attack. Maybe a dog like that would be a good thing to have around my house. A dog that would bark and rush at the door if anyone came near the house, as they had already done. I could do as Bailey's owner had done, stop at the humane society and see if there was a dog that was territorial. A dog that I could leave in the house when I was gone.

Now I was filled with eagerness to find out how to construct an IED. And when I did, I would fashion one and Earl Anthony Winslow would be the recipient. He would not know what hit him and when the confusion settled he would know that I was the one. That the egret had struck, its long yellow beak had pierced him and there was no way that he could remedy this, no way that he could buy his way out of his predicament.

CHAPTER 22

Back at the house I googled, once again, the IED. But there was no formula for constructing one. There was plenty of information about how they worked, how much they had destroyed, but no list of the ingredients. The Internet told me that the parts were simple: a detonator that might be a garage door opener or a cell phone. The part of the bomb that set it off was an electrical charge or a small explosive charge. The charge itself was what did the damage and in cases like those in Iraq, they used the charge from a land mine. But there were other options, dynamite stolen or purchased, chemical explosives, and even mention of explosives that could be cooked up by somebody with the chemical knowledge. The device could be hidden in any kind of a package. Often the IEDs used on the battlefield were hidden in the dead body of an animal, or even in the dead body of a casualty. The injuries in the Middle East were no longer by rifle or mortar. They were mostly by these devices, buried on a roadway or driven to the point of explosion. Sometimes they were set off by someone watching, at other times the delivery person was blown up along with the victims. It was one thing to tell me that a garage door opener or a cell phone could be used to set off the bomb, but another to know exactly how such a device would be wired. What I needed were some blueprints. Or someone with the knowledge how such things worked. And I needed to find the explosive. I couldn't purchase dynamite. I could steal some, but I would have to find out where dynamite was kept. The Internet said that construction sites were possibilities, but it would have to be construction where they were blowing up things. Road work or tunnels, coal mines. There were no coal mines in California where I lived. What I needed was to find someone who knew how to build an IED, and that would not be easy. Still, there had to be someone out there who knew how to fashion a bomb that would blow up Earl Winslow's Mercedes. Timothy McVeigh had fashioned a bomb that blew up a whole multi-story building in Oklahoma City. McVeigh used ammonium nitrate, fertilizer, but he packed a truck full of the stuff. I needed something small enough to put in Winslow's driveway, something that could be hidden in a small package. It would take time to find the answer, but egrets have time. They stand and wait and eventually the moment comes.

CHAPTER **23**

The new job in Santa Rosa meant that I had an hour's drive in the morning, another hour at the end of the day. I took off early in the afternoon, and stopped at the Humane Society in Novato. The building resounded with barking and when the volunteer led me into the kennels, the barking increased.

"This is what we have right now," she said. We walked along the row of cages, the dogs pressing against the wires we passed. A Chihuahua, some other tiny dogs that yipped rather than barked, a big white-coated dog whose bark was a significant bass, a mixture of discarded or abused animals. We came to the last cage where a German shepherd, some-what the worse for wear, coat shaggy, did not press against the wire. It lay in the back of the cage, watching us.

"This is Grizzly," she said. "He looks calm, but he's deceptive." She moved closer, stopped and put her hand on the latch that secured the cage door and the dog bolted at her, slammed into the cage door, growling.

"He looks out of control," I said.

"No. It's a peculiarity of dogs like him. He's intensively protective of wherever he lives. If we put a leash on him, you'll find that he's quite manageable."

"You mean if I were to take a dog like that home, he would attack anyone who came to my doorstep?"

"That's the drawback with this dog. He's probably too old to be re-trained. Anyone who takes this dog will have to deal with that problem. It's one of the reasons he's still with us. A couple of times he got taken, only to be brought back because he went after visitors or the mailman or a pizza delivery boy."

"I'm looking for a dog that can be left alone in my house, frighten off prowlers."

"As long as he can't get at the prowler, he might be a good fit." She held out a leash. "You can take him for a walk. We have a big lawn area outside the back of the kennels."

She began to unlatch the door to the cage and the dog came at the door again. "Good dog," she said, reaching into her pocket for a doggie treat. She held out her hand and the dog stopped growling, sniffed at her hand through the wires. She opened the door, clipped the leash on the dog's collar, and it came out of the cage gingerly, taking the treat from her outstretched hand.

"He knows me," she said. "I'm the one who walks him. Once he gets to know who feeds him, who cares for him, he'll do what you say. But he takes a lot of getting used to." She handed the leash to me. "Out that door," she said. "If you meet other dogs, he's good with them. He's a great dog but the only problem is that territorial nonsense."

I took the dog outside. It pulled at the leash, sniffed at bushes, and was generally well mannered. It seemed a fortuitous meeting. When I got back inside I said, "What's the procedure in adopting a dog like that?"

"There's paperwork. We send somebody to check out your house. You give us some background information and if there's nothing untoward, you're cleared. There's a three hundred dollar fee. It's one of the ways we finance what we do. And there's a two-week trial period. If anything goes wrong, you can bring the dog back. You have to register the dog with a vet. There's a good one in Fairfax, where you live. And that's it."

I spent the next half hour filling out the papers, gave them a check and drove home. If all went well, I could pick up the dog in three days. The only dog I was familiar with was the puppy we bought for our daughter when she graduated from sixth grade. It was seven years old when she was killed, and my wife had given the dog to a friend of our daughter. She couldn't bear to have the dog around the house. But when the dog grew old and cantankerous, the friend gave the dog back to me and I kept it until I had to put it down. And now I would have a new dog. One that would lunge at the door the next time anybody scratched at it. If anyone did.

CHAPTER 24

I found a site on the Internet where it showed how to rig a garage door opener so that it triggered an electrical charge. The switch of a garage door motor is activated by the opener. which means that electricity begins to flow into the motor. It turned out to be relatively easy to attach a battery to a switch, press the opener and the current from the battery closed the switch. All that was necessary was to connect the switch to something that was explosive. Which, of course, I didn't have.

One of the guys on the job, working on the foundations, told me about blasting some rock for a house they had built on the ridge above Tiburon. "Big fucking ledge," he said. "Code says you got to go down eighteen inches, doesn't matter what the fuck is there, dirt or rock, so we just blew the fucker up. Laid mats over the top so we didn't spatter the neighborhood with pieces of rock."

"Where did you get the stuff to blow it up?"

"We didn't. Ken hired some company in Sacramento. They mostly do stuff up in El Dorado County, the Sierras. Roads and shit like that."

So I found out the name of the company and spent an afternoon in Sacramento. I talked to the receptionist and lied about who I was, telling her I was a contractor from Marin County who needed some blasting work done. I explained that it was a small job, some site work before a house was to be built and asked if I could speak to a foreman or somebody who could give me advice.

She gave me the name of one of the owners of the company. He was on a job at that time, up in Shingle Springs, where they were removing an old dam on a ranch. Could I come back at the end of the week? Or could he call me?

I wasn't sure what it was I was going to tell him. What I wanted to know was where I could get a couple of sticks of dynamite and a couple of blasting caps. And from my research I knew that I couldn't get them without a permit. And his company wasn't about to hand them to me. But now I knew where their corporation yard was and obviously there were things like that stored there. I needed somebody to slip those things to me for a fee. Surely there was a worker who would be willing to do that. But only if I gave him a story that satisfied him. Something that showed I had a reasonable use for them, not something that could cause trouble. The blasting caps I could probably get from someone online, but the sticks of dynamite were something else. Still, I was determined to bring my project to an end that would result in Earl Winslow being severely damaged. If Detective Fuller managed to link me to that killing in West Marin, then I would be isolated, and Winslow wouldn't be any wiser. If he tracked me down, he would find me already removed, and that was almost more than I could think about. No, I would find some way to get the explosive. Even if I had to steal it.

The owner of the company called me the next evening. What did I have in mind? He asked.

I explained that it was a small job, a ridge on a lot had to be removed and it was too difficult to get heavy equipment up. "We do that sort of thing all the time," he said. "You want me to come down and take a look at it, give you a bid?"

"Not just yet." We chatted a bit more but it became apparent that there was no way that I could get to one of his workers and forge a deal. What I would have to do would be to go back to Sacramento and steal what I needed from his corporation yard.

"I'll get back to you," I said.

Now what I needed to do was make an evening run to Sacramento, somehow get inside his company yard and find the explosives. They would be locked up. But according to my research, dynamite wasn't unstable unless it was carelessly stored, and the company in Sacramento wasn't likely to be careless with explosives. Packed in cases, it is easily transportable, and as long as the cases weren't subject to extreme temperature changes, there was no danger in removing some of it.

I drove to Sacramento in the evening traffic, found the company yard and parked down the street. It was an industrial area and the street lights were few and far between. I waited for a while to make sure no one was staying late and then, when it neared midnight, I got out of my car. I looked carefully to make sure there was no one on the street before, using a pair of bolt cutters, I snapped the padlock. I pocketed the padlock. No point in leaving a chopped up padlock as proof that they had been broken into. I slipped inside and went through the sheds until I finally found what I was looking for, a shed that had a warning sign on the door. NO ADMITTANCE EXCEPT FOR AUTHORIZED PERSONS was emblazoned on a hand-lettered sign. This had to be the repository for explosives. There was a padlock on this shed, too, and I cut it off. Inside were cases with the label Dyno Nobel, the company that manufactured the dynamite here in the U.S. That much I had garnered in my Google search.

I opened a box. Two sticks of dynamite wouldn't be missed. I took them, searched until I found the storage of blasting caps, selected two electrically powered ones, slipped back out and put a new padlock on the door. Whoever tried to open it with the old key would be frustrated. Eventually they would cut the lock off, but they would put it down to a mix-up in locks, not to a burglary. I did the same at the front gate. Of course the new locks would raise eyebrows, but they wouldn't connect those locks to me. I drove back to Fairfax, arriving well after midnight. I put the contraband in the garage, nestled in a box of old newspapers. Now all I had to do was assemble my IED.

CHAPTER 25

The Humane Society called me and told me I had been cleared to pick up Grizzly. I drove out to the facility and the same volunteer woman gave me a handful of doggie treats. "When he rushes at the gate, pause. Tell him he's a good dog. Hold out your hand. Let him sniff it through the wire. You saw me do that. And open the door slowly, let him take the treats. You may have to do it two or three times. Then you clip the collar on him and he's good to go. Good luck with him," she said as she gave me the leash.

She was right. And within half an hour, Grizzly was sitting in the passenger seat of my Toyota, surveying the traffic in front of us

"Good dog," I said, holding out more treats. He took them without biting my hand, a slow nibbling with his lips and tongue. At home I fixed a bed for him out of old blankets, put water in a bowl and put some kibbles I had bought in another bowl. We settled in, and I felt good. Things were falling into place.

The next few days we established a routine. I walked him in the early morning, filled his bowl, stroked him, left him, locking the door, and drove to the job in Santa Rosa. When I got home and put my key in the door I could her him rushing at the door, growling, a low guttural sound that was frightening. I opened the door a crack, said "Good dog, good dog," and held out my hand with some doggie treats. The growling stopped and his muzzle appeared in the crack. Within a few days he was used to me, and even though he continued to rush the door, he quickly knew that there were goodies to be had when I opened the door

The instructions I found on the Internet told me that the blasting cap was to be immersed in the dynamite, and the wires attached to it, everything packed carefully. If I wanted more damage, I should pack ball bearings or nails around the dynamite so that they would be hurled by the explosion into whatever they came in contact with. I spent time in the garage, Grizzly at my feet, carefully measuring the dynamite, very carefully packing things into a package not much bigger than a newspaper. I had stolen a *New York Times* from a driveway and used the blue plastic bag to cover my creation. All that was left was for me to test out my device. It had not been difficult, but the Internet research had told me that it had been done by relatively unsophisticated men in the Middle East. When I was finished, my device looked like a Sunday *New York Times* ready to be dropped on someone's driveway.

What I had to do was take one of the two devices up into the hills away from where it could be heard, find an isolated spot and detonate it, using my garage door opener, to see if I had done everything correctly. If I had, the next step would be to deliver the *New York Times* to Earl Winslow, so that when he drove out of his gate, he'd be sent to oblivion.

I drove up the Bolinas Road past the Meadow Club, the green golf course shining below me, and then on to where the road began to wind through hairpin turns toward the top of the Bolinas ridge. I stopped at a curve where I could hike up into the brown grass, past the oak tree line, until I was on the far side of the ridge. Any sound would be muffled by the hills; I laid my device on the ground and retreated until I was perhaps thirty yards away. I crouched down so that whatever happened would not hurl anything at me and pressed the button. Nothing happened. Too far away, I thought. I crawled on my stomach until I could see the package. I slid over until I was behind the trunk of a sizeable oak tree. I held the garage door opener out to one side and pressed the button again, and suddenly there was a tremendous blast, leaves from the oaks floated down, crows rose screaming in the air. I raised my head, looked at where I had placed the package. A monstrous hole had appeared where I had left it. And I imagined Winslow's Mercedes upside down, the windows shattered, Winslow and his driver in pieces. It was one of those scenes right out of the newsreels, soldiers blown up by a hidden device, and I could imagine his cries, the pain that he was feeling, and I was pleased with myself. The crows had settled again, and there were intermittent squawks and the hills descended into silence. I would deliver the *New York Times* to Earl Winslow's driveway and when his Mercedes came out of the gate, I would press the button of the garage door opener and finally know the completion of what I had imagined for three years. He would not be hanging upside down in the rising water, and he would not drown as I hoped he would, but his limbs would be shattered, and no amount of his money would be able to fix what I had done.

I drove back down past the Meadow Club. I turned off, parked in their parking lot and walked up to the clubhouse. At the bar I ordered a Manhattan and the Hispanic bartender made a good one, pouring it to the rim of the glass, only unlike the bartender at the Great Western, there was no leftover to fill an adjoining shot glass.

Still, it was a good drink, and I savored it. Now, I would wait, like the egret, near Winslow's driveway, and when he emerged, like the finning minnow at my feet, I would strike. My great yellow beak would impale him and he would be no more. And I would lift my wings and move on, a graceful creature who had avenged the death of my daughter, had brought justice to a scene where a coward had fled to safety. I finished the drink, left a sizeable tip for the bartender and drove back down to my little house.

CHAPTER 26

The job in Santa Rosa was almost finished. Ken said that he had more work for me. The job in Ross was still in progress, but I said no, not Ross.

"You'll have to wait for the next one," he said. "I've got one coming up in Vallejo, if you're willing to drive that far."

"No problem," I said. "Just give me a call."

Tuesday and Thursday, that's when he left his house, bound for some sort of company meeting. And on a Tuesday morning I would put the *New York Times* in his way. I continued my routine of walking Grizzly in the morning, he had become a companionable dog, lying in the evening at my feet. I became accustomed to him, and occasionally stroked his head as he lay here. No one had come to the door and he hadn't had any opportunity to charge at it. I was beginning to get used to him, a welcome companion in an empty house. I went off down to the coffee shop, leaving him to guard the house, sat at the window of the coffee shop watching the Spandex-clad bike riders and the mothers with baby strollers. I had my coffee, and counted the days. It was Friday. Saturday, Sunday, Monday and then Tuesday. I picked up some hamburger from the grocery store and some hamburger buns. Grizzly would like the leftovers. In fact, I would make him a burger without a bun. , But when I got to the door of my house and inserted my key, the familiar rush and growling weren't there. I opened the door and there, on the floor was the carcass of the dog. Its throat was slit and there was a pool of blood on the floor. I stopped, waiting to see if anyone was in my house but it was silent. Somebody had gained entrance and had killed the dog. I looked into the bedroom and it was in a chaotic state. Someone had thoroughly searched it, and I had no idea what they had been looking for. The kitchen space was the same way, pots and pans on the floor, dishes and cups broken. It was a message to me. Here we are, they had said and nothing will stop us. Not even your fierce dog. I went out to the garage and my tools were spread out, shelves stripped. But the Glock was still in my tool box in the trunk of my car. They hadn't found that. Now I was more determined than ever to do in that sonovabitch. His hired hands had come into my house and had slaughtered a dog, and if I had been there they would have slaughtered me, too. You fucking cowards, I said out loud, you killed a dog that wasn't going to harm you. You did it to send a message to me. It is an evil thing you have done. And Earl Winslow, you will go up in a shower of explosion. You will lose your limbs and you will no longer be able to fuck that pretty wife of yours. You will be either a shell in a wheelchair or a body on a slab in the morgue, I promise you that.

I got a shovel and dug a hole in the slope below the house and buried the dog. I went back into the house to begin the process of cleaning up the mess. And while I was doing it, I kept thinking of the explosion in the hills, the crater my device had left and the destruction it would wreak on Winslow's expensive car. It was not armored like the Hum-Vees in Iraq. It would shatter and the ball bearings and nails I had packed around this edition would tear through the body, ripping apart Winslow and his driver. I felt a mild disappointment that the driver would have to suffer. It was

Winslow I wanted to punish. But there was no other way. Tuesday would be the day.

CHAPTER 27

I went through the steps carefully. I would strap the package to the back of the bike, careful to cushion it with rags. I wanted to make sure that it didn't get jolted, wires come loose. I would ride the bike down the hill, pedal carefully through San Anselmo, then along Shady Lane to Ross. I would pedal carefully up Lagunitas. No, I would push the bike up the hill. Nothing unusual about that, middle-aged man pushing a bike uphill. When I got to Carmel Drive I would go to the corner just above Winslow's address. I would park the bike next to the bushes that obscured his neighbor's house. Push it back into the foliage. Unstrap the device. Walk it down to Winslow's driveway, place it in the middle of the driveway just outside the gate. There were copies of the *New York Times* in their blue wrappers on many driveways in Ross. Go back to the edge of his property where his tall hedge ended. I could tuck myself into the space between the end of his hedge and the bushes next door. There was enough space. Wait. I would hear the opening of the gate, I could see the nose of the car come out and I would press the button. The explosion would lift the car, hurl it into the air and tumble it into the street. Tumble it. Pinwheel it. It would pinwheel with what remained of Winslow inside, and I would go to my bike, ride to the top of Carmel Drive where it intersected with Canyon Road, coast down Canyon Road and when it intersected with Shady Lane, I would turn north again, retrace my route to my house while behind me the burning hulk of

Winslow's Mercedes would lie in the street and the Ross Fire Department would come and neighbors would appear and it would be done. Complete.

What did egrets do when they had speared their catch? They rose, opened their wings and flew. They tucked their heads into their shoulders (if birds had shoulders) and they rowed with their wings, stroked through the air, like long white oars in a steady beat. I would fly, too. Which meant that I had to pack things up now. Gather the tools I intended to take with me, pack a minimum of clothes and toilet articles, a good jacket, an old sweater that was a favorite of mine, empty my bank account. Convert my assets into cash before I blew up Winslow. Which meant that it would take me more than a few days. I would have to have my affairs wrapped up, cash in hand, ready to take wing when I delivered the *New York Times* to Earl Anthony Winslow.

There would be no chance to sell my house. That would take too long, was too complicated. But the rental market in Marin was hot, and I could rent my house easily for three thousand a month. I could do that within a week. Rent it furnished, ask for a first and last month's rent and a cleaning deposit. I could have seven thousand cash in hand. My savings account had another fifteen thousand in it. My checking account had a bit more than a thousand. I had a life insurance policy I could borrow against. There was more than fifty thousand there. If I took a second on the house, it would take a little more than a week to get a check. I could get another two hundred thousand, easily. I would eventually default on the loan, but the bank would have to deal with that. I would be far away, flaring my wings, settling in to a new place. Which meant that I could, within a week and a half, have a quarter of a million dollars, enough to relocate somewhere else, start over, know that Earl Winslow had suffered for his carelessness. I could even get myself a new dog.

I started by calling the Chase Bank at the Redhill Shopping Center. A banker with a smooth, well-modulated voice answered my questions about a second mortgage. "I want to put a down payment on another piece of property," I said. "I want to take out a second on my house, which is paid for. But I need the money quickly. It has to be a cash transaction, and the buyer is willing to sell if I can come up with the cash within a week. Is that possible?"

"It's highly unlikely," he said. "The bank has to get assurances about your property and details about your financial history."

"I came to you because I have a checking account with you and a savings account. Surely you can expedite things for me."

"I can try."

"Not good enough," I said. "There are companies that advertise on the television that I can get instant approval for a house loan. You're sure you can't do anything?"

"Let me call you back," he said.

An hour later he called. He had talked with someone in the San Francisco office, and if I could produce the deed to my house and the documents showing that it was fully paid for, I could get the cash within a week. I was profuse in my thanks. Now I had a schedule. A week from Tuesday would be the new date. I began to make a list of what I should pack.

CHAPTER 28

I hadn't counted on Winslow's hired thugs. That night the motion sensitive lights outside went on, illuminating my driveway and the slope beneath the house. Someone was out there. Either that or a deer had wandered into the scope of the lights. I went to the front window and looked out. No one. I held the Glock in my hand and waited and then the bottle crashed against the front door and the gasoline inside flared up. A Molotov cocktail, hurled from the darkness. I grabbed the kitchen fire extinguisher, hoping that there wasn't somebody out there with a gun ready when I showed myself. I pulled open the door, doused the flame with the extinguisher, the white cloud smothering the flame. The door was scorched, and the porch had a black burned patch but the fire was out. I was no longer safe in my house. I needed to hold out for a week, finish my plan to punish Winslow and flee. I spent the rest of the night half awake, waiting to see if they came back. The next morning I was careful when I went to the garage, loaded my tools into the car, and drove to Santa Rosa. The job finished today, and I would be on my own for several days until the Vallejo job began. I sat on the back porch, sipping a scotch. I would miss this view. I was used to the green that surrounded me. I thought of the far corners of the state, Susanville where the prison was that Fuller had threatened me with. I would find a place there that was surrounded with green. And there would be mountains that I could look at.

CHAPTER **29**

The next week was filled with trips to the bank, packing my car, meeting with a real estate agent for the rental and by Friday, I had it all complete. The check for the second mortgage was due the next week. It would be after I had set off the *New York Times* in Winslow's driveway, but I figured I had a few days of grace. By Wednesday I had the check from the insurance company and the cash from my savings account. The real estate agent had a renter for me and I would meet him on Tuesday afternoon.

The weekend came and I finished packing my car. The house already seemed empty. Monday came and I got a telephone call that was suspicious. I was accustomed to calls from contractors offering discounts on home improvements, roofing companies offering to put on a new roof and recorded voices telling me that I had won a trip to the Caribbean. But this call was different. It started by calling me by name. And then it told me that I could get a new dog to replace the one that had died if I was interested. When I asked who this was, the voice said, "It doesn't matter who I am. This is a notice that you will be dealt with. You have done enough and now is the time for you to either disappear or you will find yourself in serious trouble. You will be looking over your shoulder when you go out for coffee. Park your bike in that bike rack and it will be the last thing you do."

So they knew where I lived, and where I went for coffee and now they wanted me to disappear. At least they weren't trying to kill me. Or, perhaps they were. Perhaps they were warning me that they knew my habits and it was only a matter of time.

Time to deliver the newspaper.

CHAPTER 30

Tuesday morning came. I lashed the bomb to the bike as I had planned, rode carefully through San Anselmo to Shady Lane, pushed the bike up Lagunitas road until I reached Carmel Drive, pedaled up to the top of Carmel Drive to the house just above Winslow's house. There were large bushes obscuring the house and the high hedge in front of Winslow's house bordered those bushes. I pushed the bike into the bushes as I had planned. I walked down to Winslow's driveway and placed the *New York Times* in front of the gate. I walked back to the crevice in the hedge and secreted myself.

I waited, and when I heard the gate hum, I knew that he was there, and the nose of the Mercedes showed and I pressed the button. The explosion was more than I had hoped for. It tore through the air, pieces of asphalt and concrete rained down, the body of the car was hurled into the street, and the echo of the explosion bounced back from houses and hills. Then there was no other noise, except the noise of flames as the wreckage burst into a ball of orange, thick black smoke billowing into the sky. There was no way anyone in that car had survived. Winslow was in pieces. The instantaneous blast had given him no warning, and for that I was disappointed. I had wanted him to suffer the way my daughter had suffered when the water slowly enveloped her. But it was done, I said to myself. The hulk of the car could now be seen as the rising heat took the smoke up between the trees. No amount of money would extricate Winslow from that smoldering "cauldron. He couldn't buy his way out of this one.

Done, I said to myself. I got onto my bicycle and quickly pedaled to the top of the street, turning down toward Shady Lane. I could hear the sound of a siren and knew somebody had called in the explosion. When I came to Shady Lane I could hear the fire engines rushing up Lagunitas and I turned toward San Anselmo. When I got to the center of town I parked my bike in the bike rack in front of the coffee shop opposite the city hall, ordered a coffee and sat at a table. It wasn't long before someone rushed in to announce that there had been an explosion in Ross. "Maybe a gas main blew up," he said. "Whatever it was, there's fire trucks and medics coming from all directions."

I listened to the buzz of conversations and then biked the rest of the way home. It was Tuesday afternoon. The check from Chase hadn't arrived yet. I had cleared out my savings and checking accounts, and the back of my car was packed with my tools. Wherever I went, I would be ale to find work. I sat on the porch at the back, looking at the mountain. I would miss this.

Fuller showed up at five o'clock. When I opened the door he said, "You fucking madman! Do you know what you've done?"

"What are you talking about?" I said.

"Your obsession with Earl Winslow has caused at least two more deaths."

"Winslow is dead?"

"No. His wife is. And the driver of their car. And you did it, you fucking nutcase!"

"What are you talking about?"

"You! That's who I'm talking about. You! You somehow forced Winslow into the ocean, and that kid from out there saw you or found out something about you and you shot him. Fucking killed him. And now you've fucking blown up two innocent people!"

"Winslow isn't dead?"

"No. He isn't dead. His wife is dead. The driver of his car is dead. I can't tie you to those deaths, but I will. I will track down your involvement in that kid's death and I will find out how you got the shit to blow up Winslow's car and I will pin you to the wall. I will stick the pin in your fucking insect body and stick you to the wall and I promise you that I will do it. I'm pissed off at myself for telling you about Winslow. If I had kept my fucking mouth shut, three innocent people would still be alive. I'm going to find out what your connection was with that kid, and I'm going to sweat your identity out of Winslow, who is now as determined to strike you down as you were to get to him. But I'll get what I want, and I'll find out where you got the explosive and you can bet that you're dead meat!"

He paused. Spittle was at the edge of his mouth.

"I don't know what you're talking about," I said. "When did this explosion happen?"

"You know goddam well when it happened. I'll be back. I'll be back with a search warrant and I'll find that fucking gun and I'll track down where you got the parts for that bomb and I'll make sure you go away for the rest of your life. Unless Winslow finds you first, and I'm not going to stand in his way. If he wants to hunt you down and snuff you out, I sure as hell won't give a shit!"

CHAPTER 31

I couldn't wait for the check from Chase. And I would have to cancel the meeting with the possible renter. What I needed to do was get in my car and fly. Go somewhere I wasn't known, away from Fuller and Winslow and the connections to me. I loaded the duffle with my personal possessions in the back seat. I had the fifty thousand from my insurance policy, seven thousand from my two accounts. It would have to be enough. In San Rafael I filled the tank with gas and set off up 101, turned off toward Vallejo and then took I-80 to Interstate 5. I drove north until I came to Chico, filled the car again with gas. By now it was dark. I took the road to Lassen, and by two in the morning I was past Chester, approaching Susanville. It was the corner of nowhere. Two big prisons dominated the town, and Wikipedia had told me that there were 11,000 inmates there, and half the population of Susanville worked in those prisons. I slept in the car until it was light, then sought out a better bed

I found a motel, a cheap one, and it was apparent when I got to the room why it was cheap. The woman who took my money shoved a registration form at me and when I said I didn't remember my license number, she said, "Make one up." Which I did. The room had a faded, stained carpet, threadbare sheets on the single bed and there were tiles missing from the shower. Opposite the room was a wire enclosure with several dogs in it. They were stocky dogs, and they gathered at the wire to stare at me. They looked like the kind of dogs that would grab a leg or an arm if given the chance. My room key was attached to a plastic number tag, reinforced with a piece of duct tape. What I needed to do was find new license plates for my car. Find the hulk of something abandoned or sitting on cement blocks in a vacant lot. I needed to scout out the town, find some place permanent to stay. By now Fuller would have his search warrant, he would have connected me to the Old Western Saloon and my chat with Davy. Perhaps Winslow had told him that I was the one who forced him into the sea. When he made the rounds of places with dynamite, as he surely would, that receptionist would be able to describe me. And her boss had my telephone number. But none of that mattered any more. Now I had to find a new identity, burrow into the sand, be like that sand worm that moved at the egret's feet.

Did I feel remorse at the deaths of the driver and the wife? Now Winslow had a loss, just as I had a loss. The driver was incidental damage, and I was sorry he had been a victim. But the wife didn't bother me. I hoped that Winslow loved her enough to grieve over her the way I had missed my daughter. Tit for tat, I thought.

CHAPTER 32

Susanville is a small town, at four thousand feet elevation on the edge of the Nevada border. Originally a lumber town, now its biggest employers are the two prisons on the outskirts of town. I found a small cottage behind an old Victorian house, and the woman in her seventies who lived in the house was happy to rent her cottage to me for what would have been a pittance in Marin County, "A hundred and fifty dollars a month," she said. "Is that too much?"

"No," I replied, and pressed the cash into her hand.

"So you're a carpenter?"

"Yes."

"You'll find work here. What we need is a good handyman, somebody who can put up shelves and replace a window and build some steps. Can you do those sort of things?"

"You bet."

I moved into the cottage, had a telephone installed and made a small advertisement that I pinned up on the bulletin boards at the grocery stores, a coffee shop and the hardware store. EXPERIENCED CARPENTER. NO JOB TOO SMALL. There were strips to tear off with my new telephone number. Everything was cash for me. No bank account, and I found an old truck rusting behind a service station that still had license plates. I took them, fashioned what looked like a current sticker on the corner of the plate and drove carefully.

It was the second week when Mrs. Carlson cornered me. I had already done two jobs as a handyman, neither one of them paying much, but it was a start. "A man was looking for you," she said.

"He wanted me to do a job for him?"

"He didn't say so. He said he was looking for the owner of your Toyota. He had the name wrong and I told him so. I caught him snooping around your cottage. He was a big man, maybe the biggest I ever saw, and I saw a lot of big men when my husband was alive and the mills were working. But this man was built like a truck, if you know what I mean."

"When was he here?"

"You must have gone down to the grocery store. Your car was still here, but there was no sign of you, so I guessed that you walked to the store. Yesterday afternoon."

Somebody looking for me. How could anyone know I was in Susanville? I was seven hours from Marin, and nearly three hundred miles. Then I remembered that I had gassed up the car in Chico and again that first night I was in Susanville, using my Standard Oil credit card. It was the only non-cash purchase I had made, and Winslow was the CEO of an oil company, and a few phone calls was all it would take for him to get the history of my card use. And he had somebody sniffing around. I would have to move again. And this time I would have to be more careful.

"If he comes around again, would you let me know?" I said.

"By all means. He didn't look like the kind of man who was up to any good. I had half a mind to call the sheriff."

"No, don't call the sheriff. And thanks for letting me know."

CHAPTER 33

Where to go? That was the question. Maybe over into Nevada. There were places in Nevada that were isolated, small towns connected to the mining industry and even Basque sheepherders who grazed thousands of sheep on arid hillsides. I would, once again, have to depart without notice, slip away in the night and find a place where Winslow's thugs couldn't track me down. But I wasn't quick enough. The big man showed up again.

I saw him in the driveway, standing at the street, and Mrs. Carlson's description was accurate. He was built like a truck; wide shoulders, no neck, arms that hung down his sides like big fenders, a waist nearly as wide as his shoulders, and no belly on him. Nothing but muscle. He wore oversize denims and a khaki shirt and his head was shaved clean, and gleamed in the sun. He stared at the house. I took the Glock out of the toolbox, made sure there were bullets in the magazine and chambered one of them. I crouched at the small window next to the front door and watched. He stood for a long time and then Mrs. Carlson appeared on her front porch. She called out something to the man and he turned to face her. He didn't reply. At least his lips didn't move. Then he turned and walked back up the street, away from the house. He didn't exactly walk, it was more of a roll, his legs working in short strides, his stocky body erect and solid and imposing. He was more than six feet tall, a giant of a man. No wonder Mrs. Carlson was worried. Don't call the sheriff, I said to myself. Don't bring the sheriff into this.

I set about packing things up. My tools were all in the car except for the toolbox. It only took a few minutes to fill the duffle bag. There was no point in leaving during the daylight. He could easily spot me and follow. Better to leave in the small hours of the morning. I would drive down 395 and turn into Nevada, then go north toward Contact. It would be easy to see if anyone was following me on those empty roads. And in Contact I would trade cars, buy another used car, pay cash. There had to be somebody in a town that small and isolated who would be willing to take my Toyota off my hands and, for an exchange of cash, give me something else to drive. Something without California plates.

I left a hundred dollars cash in an envelope for Mrs. Carlson with an apology for leaving without notice. Just after midnight I put my bag and the toolbox in my car. I put the Glock under the driver's seat where I could reach it. I drove out of Susanville toward the east, hooked up on 395 and drove south. There were no headlights behind me. The road was empty, but I was sure that they hadn't just let me drift off into the night without noticing. If they had gone to the trouble of tracking me down in Susanville, then they would continue to keep track of me.

At Alturas I went east into Nevada, took the highway south until I came to Interstate 80 just east of Sparks. By now it was three o'clock in the morning and the only other vehicles were the occasional eighteen-wheelers on an all-night run. Interstate 80 was easy, little traffic, and I kept the old Toyota at a steady seventy miles an hour. In Winnemucca I stopped, put gas in the car, and drove on toward Wells. I reached Wells at five, and stopped at a huge truck stop, idling big rigs surrounding me. Inside was a twenty-four hour café, and I had a trucker's breakfast, went to the toilet, splashed water on my face, and took Highway 93 North out of Wells. It was an empty two-lane road. Nothing behind me, no cars coming my way for more than an hour. Eventually I saw signs for Contact, and when I reached it, the sun was up. Contact was virtually empty. It had obviously once been a nice little town, but it was largely abandoned, empty shops, and I drove on toward Jackpot, the last town before Idaho.

Jackpot was more promising. Lots of motels and several casinos and the big lure seemed to be gaming for people who dropped down over the state line from Idaho. I found a motel for forty bucks a night, and collapsed.

The next morning I put my original license plates back on the car and I looked for a car dealer. There were none. But there was a tire shop and when I asked, the fat guy behind the counter said, "You trying to sell your car? Had a run of bad luck?"

His words were a stroke of luck. "Yes. What I'd like to do is trade down, maybe get a bit of cash in the bargain."

He took a look at the Toyota, checked the tires, asked if he could drive it. He got behind the wheel and we toured what little there was of Jackpot.

"I've got a Ford Explorer," He said. "It's got a hundred and fifty thousand on it and the four-wheel drive is broke, but the tranny is good and the engine is OK. I can give it to you with five hundred cash for this Toyota."

It was a rip-off, that much I knew. But he was used to gamblers down on their luck and I decided to play the part.

"How about six hundred?" I asked.

"No. Five hundred is my limit."

The Ford Explorer had a crack in the windshield, but the shift was smooth and the engine seemed smooth as well. The seats were well-worn. Somebody had used this vehicle heavily. Still, it had Nevada license plates, ran OK, and I would be shed of the Toyota.

"OK, I said. It's a deal."

Inside his office he got out some papers and asked to see my California license.

"Can we do this on a cash basis? Let me do the paperwork? All you have to do is file a quit claim and you're no longer connected to it."

He looked at me. "You got the papers for the Toyota?"

"All of them. Pink slip, ownership. But I'd like to keep my name out of this."

"I can do that," he said. "I'll file a lien against you for non-payment for a set of tires. You give me an address, and I'll send the letter and the car becomes mine, no questions asked. That suit you?"

"Perfect," I said. There was no doubt he had done this before.

"Is there any place I can hole up here in Jackpot for a while?"

"Not likely. You'd be better off in Twin Falls."

"How far is that?"

"Less than fifty miles."

"What about the Nevada license plates?"

"We get Idaho plates here all the time. They get Nevada plates. Nobody pays any attention."

So I went farther north. The landscape was desolate until I got into Oregon, then it began to green up a bit. The Snake River Canyon ran along the edge of the town, and the town limit sign told me there were forty-four thousand people living there. Surely it was a town where I could get lost. I drove around a bit. The Perrine Bridge, a massive steel structure spanned the Snake River Canyon and the Shoshone Falls spilled in cascades just outside of town. I stopped at a Chamber of Commerce booth on one of the tree-shaded downtown streets and asked about housing.

I found a room in a lodging house, and settled in. Two days later there was a note under my windshield wiper. "YOU CANT ESCAPE YOUR FUCKED," it read in block letters.

They had, somehow, found me. Perhaps the tire dealer in Jackpot had been paid off. Or they had put a tracking device in the Toyota and that was how they traced me to Jackpot. Whoever was doing the tracking knew their stuff.

DIEGO

CHAPTER 34

I got out my road atlas. Whoever had put the note on my windshield knew my car and the license plates. I would have to do it differently, but this time I would crawl under the car, inspect it for some sort of device that would enable them to hunt me down. I crawled under the car and began the inspection, working from back to front, carefully running my fingers into every possible place where something could be placed. And sure enough, I found a cigarette package sized device tucked into the frame, secured with some sort of heavy mastic. I carefully pried it off and crawled under the car next to mine. I stuck it onto the frame. I had no idea whose car it was and no idea where he drove it, but by the time they found out where it was, I would be long gone. I found a sporting goods store where they sold fishing licenses, hunting licenses, and basic camping gear. I bought a sleeping bag and a foam pad, a small gas stove, several canisters of gas and a set of pans, nestled inside each other like Russian dolls. I bought a Coleman lantern and another jacket, this one a thick outdoorsman's jacket. l bought a big can for water and tablets for purifying water. A young woman who worked there helped me round out my camping gear. When I was done, I knew that, with food supplies, I could stay several weeks in some out-of-the-way campground, off the grid.

That evening I pored over my maps. If I took the tiny grey-lined roads, paved and sometimes unpaved, I could go over into Oregon, go south back into Nevada and find a campground somewhere on the Marys River above Elko. There was one road that ran, straight as an arrow, south from Oregon, between two mountain ranges. An examination of the campground guide I had bought at the sporting goods store, showed several unimproved campgrounds in the National Forest there. I found one, Gance Creek, that seemed ideal. There was a turnoff to a ranch, and the road ran almost ten miles before it passed the ranch, then wound up into the mountains. The campground showed no permanent fire pits or tables, just a notification that it was open in the summer. I could go there, wait two weeks, and then go south, heading toward Colorado since it would be approaching Fall and I didn't want to end up in the snow.

I left, once again, at night. Within a few hours, I was in Oregon, turning south. The road was narrow, not much more than a wide lane, sometimes paved, often just smooth gravel that came up into the wheel wells like rifle shots. It was mid-afternoon when I got to the ranch turnoff. The roads were straight, as if they had been planned with a laser beam, mile after mile of sagebrush and buckbrush, punctuated periodically by white-faced cattle that raised their heads at the sound of the approaching vehicle. I passed the ranch, a few low-slung buildings among a grove of cottonwoods and began to climb. Gance Creek Campground was truly isolated. There was a tiny creek that meandered through bristly brush, and evidence that cattle occasionally wandered through the campground.

I set up camp, feeling satisfied with myself. My days were quiet, reading in the folding camp chair that I had bought, collecting firewood and building a fire to keep myself warm and to cook, saving the gas stove for emergencies. It was the kind of life that I had imagined spending with my daughter. She, too, liked the outdoors and I knew that she would have liked this little clearing among the scrub oaks and pines.

I was there a week when I heard the engine. I assumed it was the rancher, checking on the cattle that I had occasionally seen on the hillsides surrounding the campground. But when the vehicle pulled into the campground it looked suspiciously like the Range Rover that I had seen in Earl Winslow's garage, and the figure that stepped out of it was my giant, the extra large man who had stood in the driveway in Susanville.

How had he tracked me? Had I not found the device that enabled him to find me here in this isolated place? Had there been a second device planted on my Explorer?

"What the fuck do you want?" I shouted.

He stood, motionless, silent.

Then he spoke. "You will come with me."

"No, I won't fucking come with you. I don't know who the fuck you are and I'm not going any place with you!"

"You have no choice." He began to move toward me. He must be armed, I thought. But he intends to take me back to face Winslow. He's been hired to track me down and capture me. I was the egret in the marsh and the coyote had spotted me and was about to pounce.

I reached back to where the Glock was tucked into my belt at my back. I had not been without that gun since I had set up camp. I slept with it clutched in my hand and if I dropped my trousers to take a shit, I laid it on a rock within easy reach. I brought it around and aimed it at him.

"Take one more step and I will shoot you," I said.

"No," he said. "I don't think you will. Aiming a handgun

like that is a special art and it's highly likely that if you do pull the trigger, you will miss."

"Somebody as big as you would be hard to miss," I said as he came closer, pausing to open his jacket. I could see a gun in a holster at his waist.

"You see, we are at what might be called a standoff," he said. "But I am trained to shoot my weapon. You are not."

"How do you know that?"

"I know everything there is to know about you, my friend." He took a step and I fired. The shot missed him and he reached for his gun and I fired again, this time the bullet slammed into his shoulder and he wheeled, as if he were changing direction, then turned back to me, still drawing out the gun. I fired again, this time the gun jumping in my hand, almost jumping out of my hand, and I continued to pull the trigger until it clicked, empty and he stopped, bent over, clutched at his stomach, and a grunt came from him. I had shot him again.

I stood there, waiting. He was on the ground, on his side, and I knew that I had done great damage to him. And he was surprised that I had done so, had not expected me to be accurate, had expected that he would capture me and drag me away, only he was struggling with the pain and I stepped forward. I leveled the gun at his head, not unlike the way I had aimed the gun at the head of the truck driver in West Marin.

'No," I said. "You will not be taking me away," and I pulled the trigger again. The gun did not fire and I realized that I had emptied the magazine. I went over to the Explorer, reached under the driver's seat and got out the carton of cartridges, carefully filling the magazine again. I went back to where he lay, his hands still clutching at his stomach. I raised the gun, pressed it to the side of his head and pulled the trigger. A hole appeared in his temple and his head slammed back against the ground. "And you were wrong. I was quite willing to shoot you. And I had enough shots to do the job, even though I am shitty at aiming." The gun was warm in my hand.

It was difficult to drag his body to the edge of the campground. He must have weighed three hundred pounds. I got out my new camp shovel, the one I had used to make myself a latrine, and began to dig. It was not a deep hole. There was no point in making it deep, only deep enough to discourage foraging animals from dragging his body into view. I pushed his body into the hole. I filled up the hole and I gathered stones from the campground to cover him, and had myself a scotch. Now I had a new vehicle, a good one, a black Land Rover with four-wheel drive and the full rhino gear, something that would go anywhere. I could leave my Ford Explorer here at the campground and eventually the rancher would discover it and it would be registered to someone who had sold it to that tire dealer in Jackpot and I was in no way connected with that transaction. Unless the tire dealer got co-opted by the police, but I had the feeling that he was the kind of man who said little to the police. Still, it would be a long time before Winslow found out that his thug was dead and his car was gone, and I could convert that car into a new one easily.

This body didn't bother me any more than the body of Winslow's wife. He was a hired thug, and he would just as easily have killed me. There was no right or wrong about what the egret killed. It stabbed at whatever it needed to ensure its own survival. And that was what I was doing. I covered up the rocks that were piled on the giant's body, tamped the dirt down and made my dinner, a can of beans that I opened and leaned against the coals, and two hot dogs that I put on sticks and roasted over the coals. Hot dogs and beans. Basic food. Probably not something on the menu at 221 Carmel Drive in Ross. But at 221 Carmel Drive in Ross, Earl Anthony Winslow was eating alone. Just as I was. I had taken the giant's gun from his body and his wallet and keys. There was a driver's license in the wallet and some cards that told me he worked for a detective agency in San Francisco. The gun was more complicated than mine, and I had taken the holster as well. I tucked them both under the driver's seat of the Range Rover. I took the Glock that I had used and tucked it, too, under the seat. I would dispose of it later. I had a new weapon and no one would be able to connect me with the killings I had done. I broke camp, packing my things neatly on the back of Winslow's car.

How appropriate, I thought. This one probably cost as much as that fancy Mercedes that I had blown up. Had he bought a new one? Or was he driving his wife's little yellow Porsche? There was the distinct possibility that the giant had told someone where he was going and when he didn't check in, someone would be sent out to check on him. So I didn't have any time to lose. I left the keys in the Explorer. When the rancher found it, he might very well simply appropriate it, which would simplify my life. I would drive Winslow's Range Rover to Elko and then beyond, into the Great Basin, and end up in Colorado. I would abandon the car and get myself a new used car and, once again, disappear. Only this time there wouldn't be anyone to put a tracking device in the chassis of the car that I bought. This time I would be careful to pay only cash. This time I would, like the egret, find a new marsh where there weren't any coyotes and Winslow would continue to eat alone.

CHAPTER 35

In Elko I had a meal in a Basque restaurant, the lamb spilling over the edge of the plate, more food than one person could be expected to eat. The bartender, a young woman, told me that her grandfather had been a Basque sheepherder who had walked the thousand miles with a thousand sheep over the Sierras from Los Angeles. She made me a really good Manhattan, and I slept on the far side of the railroad tracks that bisected Elko, comfortable in the roomy rear of the Range Rover.

The next morning I went south on Highway 229, over what was called the "Secret Pass." The Ruby Mountains were to my right, rising pale and indistinct in the morning light. I passed through low-lying hills, grasslands, sagebrush, and in the early morning light it was more than beautiful. I stopped midmorning at a point where the road crossed over a small stream. I got out of the Range Rover and stood on the bridge, looking down into the water. I still had the giant's pistol and I realized that if they caught me with it, it would tie me to his death. Even so, my car was still back at that campground and it wouldn't take much for them to discover his body. Still, I had my Glock and I didn't need his pistol. I went back to the car, got the gun out from under the driver's seat and went back onto the bridge. I threw the gun into the deep water beneath the bridge, got back into the car and drove on. I threw the giant's wallet out into the sagebrush on a long stretch, and it disappeared .

At noon I ate the rest of last night's meal, saved in a small cardboard carton. I opened the windows of the Range Rover and lay in the back and slept. When I awoke, it was beginning to get dark. I drove further toward the Secret Pass, and suddenly was stopped by a huge herd of sheep that covered the highway. Dogs ranged at the sides of the herd, nipping at them, and they flowed like a white river across the road. At the rear was a small pickup truck towing a boxy wagon. The driver waved at me, and when he swung onto the road, his arm came out his window, and he waved to me again. At first I thought he was waving me on, but then I realized he was motioning me to follow him.

He pulled off the road, stopped, and climbed out of his truck. He whistled, and the dogs dashed to the front of the herd, slowing the sheep, ranging back and forth until the flock was stopped. The dogs sat at the perimeter, pausing only to get up and nip at a vagrant sheep. The man motioned to me to join him.

"I am Diego," he said. "These are my sheep, but I suppose you figured that out. Join me for supper, unless you are in a hurry to get to some destination."

Why not, I thought. I watched while he unhitched the boxy trailer and opened it up. It was a caravan with a bunk inside, shelves filled with cooking utensils and foodstuffs.

"You will have dinner with me," he said. "It is a welcome thing to have dinner with someone else. All the company I have is four dogs and a thousand sheep. My father and I walked sheep from Hallelujah Junction. Do you know where that is?"

"It's over on the California border. That's a long way."

"Yes, if you are driving to see your grandmother. But to us, it is just one day after another." He set up a portable stand that held a grill, brought wood from a bin at the side of the wagon and started a fire.

"We will have lamb for our meal," he said. "I will pick sage to flavor it. It will be just like my father made for me. And no doubt what his father made for him."

I watched while he tended the fire and when it was going well, he brought out two folding chairs.

"I have some scotch," I said. "Would you like some?"

"An improvement over the Spanish wine that I have."

He got out two glasses and I got the bottle of scotch from my duffle bag.

"Where are you going?"

"I have no particular destination."

"You have a fine machine to travel in," he said, motioning with his glass at the Range Rover.

"Actually, it's not mine. I'm simply using it."

We drank silently and the sun went off the Ruby Mountains, sliding down over the westward ridge, leaving the tops of the Rubies in light and then they were grey, and his face was lit with the glow of the burning coals. He took a package from the trailer, unwrapped it, and rose to strip some sage leaves. He rubbed the sage onto the meat, rubbed some salt and pepper and said, "It cooks slowly, which is best." He took two large potatoes, cut them in half and doused them with olive oil, laying them on the grill next to the meat. "In the morning," he said, "I make bread." He whistled and the dogs assembled out of the darkness.

"The sheep will stay where they are. Sheep are not adventurous animals." The mewing sound of the sheep echoed in the darkness.

"What is the most pressing thing in your life?" he said. "That is a question I ask everyone."

Perhaps it was the scotch. Or the isolation. Or the easy-going manner of this old man. For some reason I wanted to tell him what I had done.

"I have killed people," I said.

There was a silence.

"Were you a soldier?" he asked.

"No. I was not a soldier. But I pulled the trigger to make them die. I planted a bomb. The last one was a huge man who wanted to kill me. But I killed him instead,"

"We have all killed people," he said. "Sometimes in the old country, sometimes here, perhaps someone who has designs on our sheep. And sometimes it was not known to us that somebody died because of our carelessness. You are not alone in this affair. " We sat in silence, the sound of the sheep punctuating the darkness. I dozed off, woke when he whistled at the dogs. They scattered into the dark. "They will gather the sheep into a tight knot," he said. "They will stay that way during the night unless something comes at them, perhaps a coyote. The dogs will know about it."

He lifted the piece of meat, cut off a slice with a knife that he withdrew from a scabbard at his belt. He offered it to me. It was delicious.

"The sheep," he said, "They do not demand much. If I find a sheep that the others will follow, then it is easy. My dogs are faithful and I do not have very many thoughts during the day."

He had said nothing else about my admission.

"Are the sheep ever silent?"

"Sometimes. When that happens, the dogs and I are on alert. Something approaches."

"Sort of like a silent alarm? And then what do you do?"

"I listen. I listen for words that come to me, words that tell me that I am doing what I should do. Words that say, yes, you can tend these creatures and protect them from the vagaries of the world. That is all I require. Sometimes you do the things that are required. You do not seem to be a man I should be afraid of."

"I have no grudge to settle with you."

"But you had one with someone."

"Yes.

"I will not judge you. It is enough that I bring the sheep back to the owner in the fall without too much loss. Some of them die. But death is part of what I do."

After that we did not speak of what I had admitted. We finished eating; I crawled into the Range Rover and slept. I did not wake and I did not dream.

I slept well and in the morning I watched while he baked bread in a Dutch oven propped next to the rejuvenated fire. We ate the bread with honey from a small jar that he produced and there were bits of the succulent lamb from the evening meal. I asked him if he had a gun.

"No," he said. "I have the dogs. They are enough."

I took out the Glock and held it out to him.

"Take this," I said. "You can do with it what you want, sell it, keep it, use it. Throw it off in the sagebrush. It makes no difference to me. I want nothing else to do with it."

He contemplated the weapon, and when I placed it in his hand he continued to look at it, detached, as if it were a piece of meat or a slice of bread, something that had no more significance that the biscuits we had for breakfast.

When I left he wished me luck. The sheep had spread out over the hillside.

It was just outside Lamoille that the Nevada highway patrol cruiser came up behind me and turned on his lights. In the rear view mirror I could see the throbbing blue lights and I thought, have I been driving too fast? Did I do something to attract his attention? The voice from his cruiser came from a loudspeaker. " Get out of your vehicle. Keep your hands visible. Turn and face the vehicle and place your arms on top of the vehicle, hands flat on the surface."'

An officer stepped out from behind the driver's wheel, leaning over the open door, a pistol in his hand, aimed at my car. I thought briefly of jamming my foot on the accelerator, outrunning him, but I knew, immediately, that it wouldn't work. I was fucked. Just as the note on my windshield had said.

I opened the door, stepped out and the officer shouted, "Slowly. Hands where I can see them!"

I did as he asked, turned and faced the car and, put my face against the smooth black surface, put my hands up on top of the car, palms down. He approached carefully, a step at a time, and when he was behind me, he told me to bring my hands down behind my back and suddenly I was handcuffed.

CHAPTER 36

At the California state line there was a Marin County sheriff's cruiser waiting, a plain white Ford Crown Victoria with a green stripe down the side. Detective Fuller stepped out and came to the Nevada cruiser where I was being held.

He leaned in the window and said, "You thought you could get away with it, didn't you?"

I did not reply. He motioned to the officer that sat next to me and he slid out, reaching back to pull me out of the car.

"Did you think you could get away with it?" he asked again.

I did not reply. There was no point. Somehow Fuller had marshaled all of his forces, found me, and now I was at his mercy. He had broadcast the description of Winslow's car and it had been my downfall. I had seen egrets at the side of the highway on the Central Valley, struck by cars. Their bodies lay, a white blot beside the road, and I knew that I would, too, become one of those white, lifeless bodies.

I was put in the back seat of the cruiser. Fuller sat in the front passenger seat and a young deputy was the driver. Once inside, Fuller leaned over and spoke to me through the wire grid that separated the front seats from the back.

"I've got you dead to rights. I've got the desk clerk at the Tomales Bay Lodge who tells me that David Lansdale came to the lodge and asked for your address. And I have you registered at the lodge the day Winslow went into the ocean. I have Winslow telling me how you forced him at gunpoint to go into the water. I have the receptionist in Sacramento who remembers you posing as a contractor, asking about blowing something up. And her boss says he talked to you on your phone. And there's a missing detective who was driving that car you were driving. I will find that gun of yours and I will match it to the slug we took out of the Landsdale kid's head and you will end up on death row."

But he didn't have my Glock gun. It was in the hand of an old man surrounded by sheep, away from that campground and there was very little chance that anyone would ever find it.

"How did you find me?" I asked.

"His agency traced him by GPS. And when his car left the campground and your car stayed there, they put out an alert to find his car. That's when Winslow called me. You traveled south and that was all they needed. My guess is that you left another body behind. Which we'll find. You're under arrest for the murder of David Lansdale and for the murders of Pamela Winslow and Arthur Ferris. I'll add the other stuff as I go along. You have the right to remain silent. If you do speak, anything you say may be used against you in a court of law. You have the right to an attorney. If you can't afford one, an attorney will be provided. Do you understand those rights?"

I nodded.

"Say yes or no," he said.

"Yes."

He turned to face the road ahead. "Let's go," he said to the driver and we set out over Donner Pass. Fuller didn't speak to me again during the trip. It was evening when we got to the Marin County jail. I was booked into the jail, my belt and shoe laces were taken along with my wallet and watch. I was given a one-piece orange jail suit to wear and put in a cell. YOUR FUCKED, the note had said. There was no doubt about that.

CHAPTER 37

Things moved like clockwork. They offered me a public defender but I hired my own lawyer, a smooth-faced man who made a habit of defending people who were, as I was, fucked. He visited me at the jail and asked me if what they were charging me with was accurate.

I said nothing,

"You must understand," he said, "that whatever you tell me is privileged."

"I understand," I said. "I prefer not to say anything."

"If I am to defend you, I need to know everything. Things you keep back make it impossible for me. I have to create a story that will cause doubt or cast a different light on what you did. But refusing to tell me the details puts handcuffs on me. I will be as shackled as you are," he said, pointing at the chains between my ankles.

So I told him. He took notes and when I was finished, he said, "What they have is circumstantial. Make no mistake, people get convicted on circumstantial evidence. But they don't have anything that will directly connect you to those crimes. They have no witnesses. They have no physical evidence. What they have is a chain of events that points a finger at you, All it would take is one juror who decides that it isn't conclusive. Beyond all reasonable doubt. That's what the judge tells them. But they have your attempt on Earl Winslow. You forced him into the sea at gunpoint, but he didn't drown. They have no direct evidence of any bomb, no fingerprints, no residue to tie you to that explosion. Yes, you bought the same caliber gun as the one that killed two men. But thousands of people buy such a gun. Yes, you showed up at a place where explosives are stored and there was a subsequent break-in, but no one saw you steal dynamite and there's no physical evidence that the theft was yours. You were arrested driving the vehicle of a man who was shot to death. It's possible that you came across the vehicle and exchanged your worn out car for his. There's nothing to connect you with his death, other than a suspicious coincidence. Your actions are suspicious. But you can't get convicted of suspicious actions."

He paused. He tapped his pen on the table, then said, "I take that back. A jury could decide that it was you. I would believe it. The chain of circumstances is believable. Juries do that sort of thing. They sometimes even defy logic. So it's not a slam dunk for the DA. But he knows what I will do with this, and he knows what happens when a juror decides that it isn't ironclad. and my guess is that he'll go for what he can easily get. Which is why a bargain is possible."

"What kind of a bargain?"

"422 PC, threat of bodily harm. It's either a misdemeanor or a felony, but he'll go for felony. That way he can put you in prison. The threat to Winslow was real, sustained, certainly not vague and he had reason to fear for his safety. The fact that he was a good swimmer is irrelevant. You didn't know that. You forced him into that dangerous surf with the intent that he drown, and under those circumstances, it's a reasonable assumption you wanted him dead."

"So I'll ask for that. As a felony, it's four years, plus one for the gun. If you keep your nose clean, you won't do the full five years. The other deaths remain open cases, so if they ever find direct evidence, they'll charge you with those deaths. But right now, they'll go for what they can get. Five years for sure is better than a hung jury."

"Doesn't it bother you that I would skate on four deaths?"

He tapped the pen again, a kind of Morse Code that only he understood.

"I don't get bothered by anything any more. I've dealt with shitbags who make you look like Mary Poppins. But these other cases will remain open, and there's no statute of limitations on them. Fuller is a pit bull; he'll clamp onto your leg and chew until it comes off. And there's nothing I can do about that. You're going to look over your shoulder for the rest of your life. You'll find Fuller in your rear view mirror no matter which way you turn."

CHAPTER 38

The DA reluctantly agreed to the bargain. Fuller came to see me again. "You think you got away with it. But I will get you if it's the last thing I do. I will be clutching an old man's walker, shuffling along the courtroom corridor with the evidence in my hand."

Once again, I said nothing.

"You're getting a free ride, "he said. "I know you pulled the trigger on two of those deaths and I know you set off that fucking bomb. But I don't have the smoking gun, as they say on television, and you've kept your fucking mouth shut and I hope you get offed in prison. I hope you do something that will get you on the wrong side of somebody and they will find your body in your cell. We found the body of that detective and he was shot with the same nine mil that killed the kid in West Marin and I know you did it. And I will search for that gun until I find it. I will search for it until I am an old man. I will retrace your footsteps and sooner or later that gun will surface. "

I kept silent. Like the egret, I waited. I was motionless. I stood at the edge of the water and waited. Nothing could make me move or speak. Nothing that Fuller said would make me say anything, and he sat there on the other side of the glass and said, "You're a fucking evil person. You blew up two human beings and you shot two others. All in the name of vengeance. Your daughter is dead. It was an accident. Can't you fucking get that through your head?"

I remained silent.

"You left a man you never met and a beautiful young woman in pieces in a smoking wreck that caught fire. What makes that young woman different from your daughter? She, too, had parents. They are, like you were, devastated by what happened. I know you meant to blow up Earl Winslow, but you didn't. He sits down to breakfast every morning, like he's done all his life. And you shot that kid in West Marin. I have no idea why, but I'm guessing that he had something on you and you decided to shut him up. Just like that. Close his mouth forever. Somewhere along the line, that part of your brain that tells you, this is the wrong thing to do, got wiped out. Just like a wet cloth on the blackboard at school. Wiped clean. So you could do your evil deed. Who the fuck do you think you are?"

I am the egret, is what I think I am, but I didn't say that to Fuller.

I stayed in my cell in the Marin County jail while my lawyer worked out the details. It took some time and the DA wasn't happy but the outcome meant that I was bound for prison and that was enough. Then I was transferred to San Quentin to wait for transportation to another prison. I would go off to High Desert in Susanville because my crime was not serious enough to warrant a place like San Quentin or Soledad. I had used a gun, and that was what put me in High Desert with others who had used a gun, in marital disputes or arguments or holding up a 7-Eleven, but none of them had been convicted of killing anyone. The irony of me ending up in Susanville was not lost on me.

THE STRIKE

CHAPTER 39

I was taken to San Quentin by two sheriff's deputies in a sheriff's car, shackled at the ankles, handcuffed, wearing the orange pullover jail jumpsuit. We went down Highway 101 to the turnoff to the Richmond Bridge, then off at the last exit toward San Quentin. I had driven past this exit countless times. We went through a village of small houses, the bay on our left, came to the gates where armed guards waited. The sheriff's car was logged in, the deputies showed their IDs and the papers regarding me and we drove into the prison. The ancient stone walls towered above us and I thought, *here I am, about to be locked away and Earl Winslow is having his morning coffee and, no doubt, a croissant from the Rustic Bakery in Larkspur, and somebody is adding hot coffee to his cup.* I was processed much the same way I had been processed at the San Rafael jail, stripped naked, every part of my body examined, sent in to shower, was given a new orange jumpsuit and re-shackled. I was led by San Quentin guards to the holding cell where I found a single iron bunk fixed to the wall, and a seatless toilet.

I spent two days in that lockup before the guards took me to the bus that would take me to High Desert. There were six other inmates making the same trip. The bus was small, space in the back for a dozen seated people, a heavy wire wall that separated the cargo space from the driver with a door in it and a heavy padlock. We were ushered in from the back, seated, then a shackle was placed between our handcuffs and the frame of the seat we were sitting in. Nothing was left to chance. The driver waited, his door open, smoking, and then a guard got into the passenger seat. He was a heavy-set man, buzz cut, wearing a holster and a radio belt. He turned to look at us.

"You guys ready?" he asked.

There was a general mumbled assent.

"Gonna be a long trip," he said. "I assume everybody took a leak before you got in. No stops. Six hours. You eat when you get there." He turned to face the windshield. "Let's go," he said to the driver, and we pulled out of the San Quentin prison yard, went through the village, turned onto the Richmond bridge and were over the water of the bay within minutes.

Last look at the bay for a long time, I thought. Nobody was talking. Because there were only six of us, each prisoner had an aisle seat. By the time we got to Vacaville an hour later, the guy across from me leaned over and said, "What they got you for?"

I said nothing. I was not in the mood for small talk with someone who was going off to prison. Of course, I was going off to prison. I was going off to prison in a grotty prison bus and Earl Winslow no doubt had a new Mercedes. He would find another attractive wife and the hole in his driveway had, no doubt, already been filled. I had failed to strike quickly. I had taken my eye off the prey, and he had escaped. Shortly after Vacaville we turned off onto northbound I-505, the freeway that would connect with I-5 and take us north to Red Bluff. I knew this journey, had taken it myself not that long ago.

We were passing through the rice fields west of Colusa when one of the prisoners near the rear exit began to moan.

He tried to clutch at his stomach with his hands, but the shackle kept him from doing so. He slumped, head on his chest and the guy sitting opposite him shouted at the guard in the front seat.

"This guy's sick," he called out. The guard didn't respond.

Now the prisoner was sagging into the aisle and he vomited, a rush of stuff that was red, as if he were vomiting blood. No telling what he had eaten that morning, but if it was the same food I had been given, there was nothing that should have shown up red.

"He's really sick!" the other prisoner shouted. The guard turned, saw what had happened and said something to the driver. The bus pulled over to the shoulder and the guard unlocked the door, crouched and came through.

At that point what I did was not thought out. It was purely reflex, and when I thought about it later I linked it to the quick stab of the egret's beak. As he passed me I reached out with my free hand and grabbed his weapon, wresting it from the holster. It came free and the guard whirled, but I had the pistol pointed at his gut.

"Unlock me," I said.

"You're fucked if I do," he said.

"No," I said. "You're fucked if you don't. I've killed four people. I don't want to kill you but I won't hesitate. And your life isn't worth some shitbag like me taking a hike. You unlock me and I leave this bus and you keep on living."

The others in the bus were shouting.

"Shoot the fucker," someone shouted. "Get his keys."

"Unlock me," I said. "I go and the rest stay where they are."

He fumbled with the knot of keys attached to his belt. He unlocked the shackle that held me to the seat.

"Now the rest," I said, pointing at the shackles on my ankles. He bent, unlocked the rings around my ankles and the chain slipped off. He unlocked the handcuffs and they fell to the floor. The driver was on his phone to someone and I went through the opening to the front seat, grabbed the phone, opened the passenger door and threw the phone into the field. "When I get out," I said. "You drive. Don't look back. Leave me here."

He said nothing, I slid out the door and the bus started forward. I ran to the fence that separated the freeway from the frontage road that ran parallel to the rice fields. I was over it quickly, and turned to watch the bus growing smaller.

A pickup truck came toward me and I stepped into the middle of the frontage road, waving my arms. The truck slowed, came to a stop as the driver peered at me. What was a man in an orange jumpsuit doing on this farm road?

I went to the passenger side, lifted the guard's pistol and yelled at the farmer as I jerked open the passenger door. "Don't move a muscle!"

I slid into the seat. "Drive," I said.

He didn't move, and I shouted at him," Drive the motherfucking truck," He put it in gear and we moved slowly off.

"Turn here," I said, pointing at a dirt road that led between two rice fields.

I told him to stop, get out of the truck, and I forced him to take his clothes off. He stood there, nearly naked, overweight, his skin pale except his neck and wrists where the sun had browned him. I pulled on his trousers and shirt, laced his boots on.

"I won't take your truck far," I said. "You'll get it back."

"You escaped from jail," he said.

"In a manner of speaking."

"What did you do?"

"It doesn't matter. What's done is done. But I have un-finished business to attend to."

I climbed into the truck, started it, and backed out of the dirt road onto the frontage road, leaving the farmer standing in his shorts and socks on the dirt road. There was an egret behind him, tall, a white brush stroke against the green of the rice. It was, I thought, a good omen. There would be po-lice coming soon. I took the first turn toward Colusa, drove, looking for the entrance to a ranch. It was midday. With any luck the men would be out tending whatever they tended in these flat fields of rice and straw. But there would be wom-en and cars.

At the first ranch turnoff I drove in, turned off the en-gine, got out of the truck and went toward the house. A woman wearing a plaid apron came to the door.

"Can I help you?" she asked.

"Yes," I said. I took the pistol out from the voluminous pants pocket.

"Oh!" She said. It was a small exclamation, as if I had showed her something valuable, like a jewel or a necklace. "Oh!" she said again, not moving.

"I'm not going to hurt you," I said "Are you alone?"

She shook her head.

"Children?"

"They're at school. Only Maria."

I gestured with the pistol and she retreated into the

house. I followed and there was Maria, a stocky Hispanic woman who looked at me and the pistol and said, "Por favor. No me mates. Yo tengo hijos."

"No," I said. "Nobody gets hurt if you do what I say. And nobody gets touched. I want a car. I want to use your car and I want to leave that truck here."

"It belongs to Bill Jackson," the woman said.

"He's OK. I left him up the road. What I want is your car. And I'm going to tie the two of you up so that you can't call the sheriff. I need a head start."

"My husband will be here shortly."

"I doubt it. I think you'll be here by yourselves for several hours. And by then I will be somewhere else."

I was strangely calm, as if this had all been planned, and I was carrying out a scheme that had been thought out.

"Sit," I said, motioning to the wall behind them. "I need something to tie you up with." I wanted something soft, something that would not scar their wrists and ankles. I had enough of handcuffs and shackles.

"Where do you keep your sheets?"

She motioned toward a closet at the edge of the room. I opened it, took out a sheet and tore it into strips. I bound their wrists tightly, then bound their ankles. The Hispanic woman was quiet, as if she had been through some ordeal that was not that different from what was happening now.

"Where is the car?" I asked.

"In the shed. The keys are on the kitchen counter."

Within minutes I was driving east on the two-lane highway toward 99. It was not the road someone would choose to flee on, but 99 led south toward Davis and eventually onto I-80 and the Bay Area. With any luck I would have an hour's head start and that would get me into the horrendous traffic on the freeway leading into the Bay area, and it would be almost impossible for the highway patrol to single out a car. It would be four lanes wide, clogged bumper to bumper with the evening traffic and I could lose myself in that confusion.

At Vallejo I took the turnoff to Highway 37, across the top of the bay. It was two lanes and chancy but if I made it all the way to Marin I could abandon the car. And find another way to do what I now knew I had to do.

There were egrets in the marshes on both sides of Highway 37. An extraordinary number of them. It was a good sign. When I turned off onto 101, I pulled into the parking lot of Rickys Restaurant. I would commandeer another car here. I waited, watching the bar exit from the car and eventually a man came out, fumbling with his keys, He unlocked a black Lexus and I stepped out and confronted him.

"Jesus Christ!" he said. "You're stealing my fucking car!"

"You're lucky," I said, "That's all I want. Just your fucking expensive car. You can go back inside and tell them a grubby man in overalls waved a gun at you and a sheriff's deputy will show up and you can have another drink. Give me the fucking keys!"

He did.

I drove south on 101 until I came to the first San Rafael exit. I drove up Mission Avenue, took the Miracle Mile out to Fairfax and abandoned the car in the parking lot in the middle of the town. Eventually the stolen car would be linked to the carjack and when they found it in Fairfax, they would think I had come back to my house, but that wasn't my plan. When Fuller found out what was happening, and

I was sure he would, he would know where I was headed. I wanted him there.

By now it was early evening. I hiked up the hill to my house. It had been searched, that much I could see. Drawers were still open, the closet had been emptied, and my kitchen cupboards had been cleared out, everything stacked on the counter and the floor. Fuller had been there, searching for my Glock. I went to the garage, and found the same mess, tools scattered, boxes emptied, the cupboards cleared out. The birdhouses had their tops pulled off. Nice hiding place for a gun. My bicycle was still leaning against the garage.

The ride down the hill was what I knew. I nodded to a man who was walking his dog, and when I came to the bottom of the hill, there was a Fairfax police cruiser, and I came to a complete stop, waved to him and he waved back. Middle aged man on a bike, wearing overalls. Typically Fairfax. Have a good day. It took twenty minutes to pedal to Ross.

It was later now, dusk settling in. I pedaled up Lagunitas, turned off on Carmel and came to Winslow's closed gate. With any luck he would be at home at this time of day and this was where I would find him.

There would be motion sensor lights and cameras and probably hired guns. I leaned the bike into the bushes next door to his house and began to separate the branches of the bushes. If I struggled, I could worm my way into their front garden.

It took ten minutes of pushing and laboring before I emerged on the inside of the bushes. My cheeks were scratched and my hands and fingers were raw. The neighbor's garden was landscaped, lawn running down toward a grove of willows at the back, but I turned toward the wall that separated their house from Winslow's. There was a stuccoed wall between this neighbor and Winslow, but it was not a high wall. It was the kind of wall that Frost wrote about. Good fences make good neighbors. It was easy to go up over the wall into Winslow's property.

I could see the house clearly now, a huge shingled lodge with a greenhouse solarium attached to the back, a swimming pool below the house, the garage with its living quarters above it, an estate that was worthy of a man who was rich. I could see no video cameras pointing at his neighbor's house. No need for that, his neighbor wasn't likely to do him harm.

I crossed the neatly cut lawn and came to the door of the solarium. It had an aluminum door with a catch that was negligible and I was able to open it with little noise.

Once inside, I listened carefully. Music came from someplace. It would be suppertime. Supper. A word that came from my childhood. My parents came from the Midwest and dinner was at noon, a cooked meal, but supper came in the evening, much like the English tea, leftovers from the noon meal, salads and cold chicken or cuts of cold meat.

But it wasn't likely that Winslow was connected with that regimen.

I listened carefully for any other voices. The music came from a room just off the solarium, meaning that I would not have to enter any of the front rooms. I found him in his study. He was at a desk that was mahagony, a top that had an inlaid blotter of felt and he turned when I said, "Winslow."

"Who are you?"

"Your worst nightmare."

Then he recognized me. "Oh shit, you're the crazy man

who forced me into the ocean at gun point."

"That's right. It's me again."

"You're supposed to be in prison."

"Change of plans. "

"Do you want money? Is that what you want?"

"No, I'm here to remind you of something you did three years ago." He swiveled in his chair and he could see the pistol leveled at him.

"I have no idea what you want me to do," he said. He seemed collected, as if he could talk his way out of this.

"No. I don't suppose you do. It was three years ago. You came around a corner on the highway to Inverness and you clipped another car, and you sent it pinwheeling into To-males Bay."

"You've got the wrong person."

"You said that the last time you saw me. And just like that time, I have the right person. There's no point in denying what you did. The car you clipped was occupied by my daughter. She died, drowned in that water. And you simply drove on."

"You're mistaken."

"No, I'm not fucking mistaken. You know I'm not mistaken. And I want you to admit what you did or I will put a bullet in your brain."

He placed his hands on the arms of his chair.

"You want me to admit to something that I never did?"

His voice was level. I knew that he was this kind of man. I knew that he was used to talking his way out of difficult positions, lying, weaseling, using his charm. But I also knew that he was the worm at my feet, ignorant of what he was doing, confident that he could somehow work his way out of this predicament, and when I struck, he would suddenly realize that he was the intended victim.

"You drove around a curve, clipped a car, it pinwheeled into the water. That's what the man who witnessed it said. A black Ford Expedition. And you drove on and the next day you had your car repaired and you gave a fake name and a fake address. Is it coming back to you, asshole?"

He looked at me, and I realized that he was calculating how much this would cost him.

"You want me to pay for your daughter's accident?"

"No, I want you to admit that you killed her and drove away, and tried to hide the fact that you are an unscrupulous son of a bitch who thinks he can buy his way out of anything. Even the death of a young woman."

"What do you want of me?"

"I want you to admit that you did that careless act and tried to cover it up and then I will kill you."

Now he was visibly agitated.

"There's no reason to kill me. Yes, I clipped another car. I had no idea that I had done more than casual damage. You can't be serious!"

"Admit it," I said

Now I heard the other noises, cars arriving. Fuller was here. It had to be Fuller. He was the one who would know that I would be either in Winslow's house or trying to get into Winslow's house.

"The cavalry has arrived," I said.

"There are two men on this floor. They are at the front of the house, not twenty steps from here. If you shoot me, they will come running and you will be a dead man."

"You know anything about birds?" I could hear voices

now, at the front door. But they had no idea that I was in the study with Winslow.

"Not much. Why?"

"There's a bird that is a stalker. It moves silently and when it finds the thing it wants to eat, it remains motionless until the thing is right where it wants it and then it strikes. Right now I have you right where I want you. I should have done this in the first place. I want to hear the words, 'Yes, I did it. I killed your daughter. I was careless and I killed her.' Those words. Nothing else."

"I can pay you a substantial amount of money. Enough to last the rest of your life. More money than you have ever dreamed."

"You know that I will go back to prison. You contacted Detective Fuller. You put the finger on me. You know what happened. You know they sent me to prison. And somehow here I am. Right now you're trying to buy time, to keep me at bay until they come back here to tell you that I am on the loose again. So no more bullshit. Say the words."

The voices were louder and I thought I recognized Fuller's voice.

I crossed to where Winslow sat and pressed the barrel of the guard's gun against his temple. "If they come through that door, I will pull the trigger. Call out to them, tell them to stay where they are."

He hesitated and I tapped him sharply on the skull with the barrel, applying it again to his skin.

"Back here," he called loudly "I'm in the study. And he's here with me and he has a gun, so don't come in. He has a gun to my head and he says if you open the door he will shoot."

Fuller's voice was suddenly loud just outside the door.

"You know who this is," he said. "I have three deputies with me and there are two of Winslow's bodyguards. We're all armed. If anything happens to him, you're a dead man."

"That's what Winslow said," I replied. "Right now the son of a bitch is trying to buy his way out of this. He thinks a cash settlement will make everything OK. How fucking dumb is he?"

"If you want to get out of this alive, put the gun down, put your hands on top of your head and come to the door. Tell me when you are at the door. I will open the door and if your hands are on top of your head, you will remain alive. If they are not, then we will open fire. Is that clear?"

"I assume you're not clutching an old man's walker, Detective."

"You don't need to die," Fuller said. "This is another threat to a man's life and you know how that works. If he isn't hurt, then all you have to face is another threat charge and the escape from the prison bus. Your fucking lawyer will make another deal. Don't do anything foolish."

Winslow was shaking at this point, and his breath was coming in gasps.

Fuller's voice again.

"There's no need for this to end badly."

No, it would end appropriately. I pointed the gun at Winslow's waist and said, "I need a hundred dollars."

He reached for his wallet.

"Put it on the desk," I said. He placed his wallet on the green blotter.

"Now the hundred."

He unfolded the wallet and took out five one hundred

dollar bills.

"No, just a hundred."

He picked up one of the bills and held it out. I took it in my left hand, made my hand into a fist with the bill clutched in it.

"Fuller," I called out. "The clothes I'm wearing belong to a farmer near Colusa. I hijacked his truck. There's a hundred dollar bill in my left hand to pay for his clothes and his boots. You got that?"

"We can give his clothes to him."

"No, that won't work. You give him the hundred, OK?"

"OK. Now come to the door."

"Say the words," I said to Winslow.

I had the gun to his head again.

"The words?"

"Yes, say those words."

"I caused the accident."

"No, say the words. I killed your daughter."

His voice shook as he said, "Please don't shoot."

"Say the words."

"I killed your daughter."

I thought of the tall egret that stood behind the farmer in the rice field near Colusa. I could see it clearly, and I knew that it would find a crawdad in the water at the edge of the field and it would strike. Its beak would puncture the shell and it would raise its beak, toss the creature into the air and catch it so that it could swallow it whole. Then I pulled the trigger. The noise was deafening in that room and before it died the door burst open and they began to fire. I could feel the beak puncture his chest, go straight into his heart. I imagined that I was upside down in a car with water rushing in. Then it was still again.

.

ABOUT THE AUTHOR

RUSSELL HILL is the author of three Edgar-nominated novels
as well as several other books. His work has been translated into
French, German, Polish, Japanese, and Spanish, and one novel,
The Lord God Bird, had been optioned for a movie. Hill is an avid
fly fisherman, has written for outdoor magazines, and has taught
writing for forty years. He and his wife still live in California where
he has spent most of his life.

Other books *by* Russell Hill *from* Pleasure Boat Studio:

Deadly Negatives
The Dog Sox
The Lord God Bird
Tom Hall and The Captain of All These Men of Death